Alan Bennett considers himself "very handsome, very cool. Dynamite." And Duncan Stein, who has just moved to Cayuta, is a creep by anyone's standards. How could balding, antisocial, antisports Duncan be a threat to Alan? How could the whole of Cayuta High go ape over Duncan's insane newspaper, with its idiotic games of unrequited love? Could Alan possibly lose his girl to such a freak?

In a year of painful growth, Alan is confronted with a series of betrayals and reversals by adults as well as his peers, yet he emerges with a new capacity for coping—and feeling.

M. E. KERR was born in Auburn, New York, and attended the University of Missouri. She is the highly acclaimed author of DINKY HOCKER SHOOTS SMACK!, also available in a Laurel-Leaf edition. Until recently, she lived in Brooklyn Heights, but now lives in Long Island, New York.

THE LAUREL-LEAF LIBRARY brings together under a single imprint outstanding works of fiction and nonfiction particularly suitable for young adult readers, both in and out of the classroom. This series is under the editorship of Charles F. Reasoner, Professor of Elementary Education, New York University.

If I Love You, Am I Trapped Forever?

M. E. Kerr

For the U.N. on 53rd Street

Published by
Dell Publishing Co., Inc.
1 Dag Hammarskjold Plaza
New York, New York 10017

ISBN: 0-440-94320-5

First Laurel printing—March 1974
Second Laurel printing—June 1974
Third Laurel printing—April 1975
Fourth Laurel printing—December 1975
Fifth Laurel printing—December 1976
Sixth Laurel printing—July 1977
Seventh Laurel printing—March 1978

ACKNOWLEDGMENTS

The lines on page 73 are from "Love Song," by Arthur
Symons, *Collected Works,* Martin, Secker, & Warburg,
Ltd. Reprinted by permission of the publisher.
The lines on page 93 are from *Cat on a Hot Tin Roof,*
by Tennessee Williams.
The lines on page 178 are from *Sweet Bird of Youth,*
by Tennessee Williams.
The lines on page 184 are from "Maybe I'm Amazed," by
Paul McCartney, © 1970 by Maclen Music.
The lines on page 184 are from *Barbary Shore,* by
Norman Mailer, Holt, Rinehart, & Winston.
The lines on page 196 are from "The Friend of the
Family," by Fyodor Dostoyevski, *The Short Novels of
Dostoyevski,* The Dial Press.

One

My grandfather tells me that writing in the first person is like painting with watercolors: only small children and geniuses can do it well.

He says: "If you *have* to write a novel put it into the third person. Maybe that way you'll keep your objectivity, and turn out something besides a self-involved word-salad no one's interested in but your mother and me."

My grandfather wanted to be a writer himself, but all his life he's run the family business: BENNETT'S, a department store on Genesee Street.

My grandfather is an unconscious put-down artist. Some people would say he's a subconscious put-down artist, but my grandfather says "subconscious" is a vulgarity for "unconscious," and people who say "subconscious" say things like "consensus of opinion" and "irregardless."

He's not a nasty put-down artist. He doesn't say, "Alan, you stupid clown, nobody wants to read anything *you'd* write!" He says things like, "Well, it's a big undertaking. I hope you can pull it off." Or—"Just remember, you put all that time and money into the boat you were going to build, and nothing came of *that*, either."

If I tell my grandfather something great like, "I just got the lead in the senior play," he'll say, "That's fine—I hope you'll be able to memorize your lines."

Do you see what I mean?

His typical response to the announcement that I was going steady with Leah was, "Well, enjoy being the Golden Boy while you can. But remember—good looks don't last, and Cayuta, New York, isn't the world."

Essentially, this is the story of a kid who moved to our town in my senior year. It was his senior year, too. His name is Duncan Stein.

From the first day he showed up at Cayuta High, we all felt he was doomed. In fact, that became our nickname for him: Doomed.

It wasn't because he was partly of the Jewish persuasion (My grandfather never allows me to say someone's a Jew or Jewish; he insists "of the Jewish persuasion" is more polite.) We have many notable families of the Jewish persuasion in Cayuta. Once a year, Rabbi Goldman from Temple

6

Emmanuel gives the Sunday sermon at Second Presbyterian Church; once a year, Reverend Gosnell of Second Pres. addresses the Saturday congregation at Temple Emmanuel. We all live together in peace, and ignore the fact that people of the Jewish persuasion are not numbered among the members of Cayuta North Country Club (though they control Cayuta Yacht Club), and that daughters of the Jewish persuasion are not often encouraged by their parents to date the sons of Christians. No one's exactly pushing for intermarriage in my all-American little hometown.

So the fact that Doomed was partly of the Jewish persuasion (on his father's side) didn't have much to do with our feelings about him. It didn't help, either. It was just one more thing that made him different from the blessed majority.

The reason Doomed's family moved from New York City to Cayuta, on the Finger Lakes, was to set up a new business. They called it Rushing Brook Farm, because of the brook which ran through the property. But when everyone in Cayuta found out it was a place for alcoholics to recover, it became known as Lushing Brook.

That didn't help Doomed's image any, either.

He might have gotten away with being this partly-of-the-Jewish-persuasion kid from Lushing Brook, if he hadn't moved to Cayuta in his senior year of high, and if he had only had a different personality.

7

But here he was, this new kid entering a crowd who'd known each other since grade school—here he was, this enormously tall, critically skinny teen-ager, who refused to join any clubs, teams, or lunchroom cliques because, in his own words, "I don't go that route."

Another thing about Doomed: he was practically going bald, in his senior year of high school. If he'd been smart, he would have just shaved his head and pretended he was pulling a Yul Brynner . . . or else grown sideburns or a moustache to compensate for his lack of hair. But no, Doomed went around with those twelve coal-black hairs combed forward on his head, telling everyone the same thing about basketball, track, sodas at Murray's after school, et cetera: he didn't go that route.

It's picayune to mention his eyeglasses. But these are the things kids notice. We're picayune. His eyeglasses were rimless (The last person in Cayuta, New York, to wear rimless eyeglasses was old Louie Cowell, who went to his Great Reward last summer, at age eighty-three. He played the organ at Second Pres., lived with his mother all his life, and was so afraid of birds that he carried an umbrella at all times to fend away any that flew into sight.)

An outsider, partly of the Jewish persuasion, whose folks made a living drying out alkies; an emaciated-looking, aloof wearer of rimless glasses, with thinning hair—there you have Doomed in a nutshell.

I'll be expanding his profile, chapter by chapter.

My name is Alan Bennett. (My father's name is Kinney, but I've long since legally adopted my mother's maiden name.) I'm sixteen.

Now comes the hard part: to describe myself objectively in the first person, avoiding turning this into the self-involved word-salad my grandfather warned me against.

While you're reading the next few paragraphs, it may help you to remember that I'm going to get what's coming to me. Just imagine that even as I write this first chapter about myself, unforeseen clouds are gathering in the distance.

But at the beginning of this novel, I am Alan Bennett, age sixteen, and I have to come right out and tell you: I'm *the* most popular boy at Cayuta High. Very handsome. Very cool. Dynamite.

Probably the best way to handle this whole embarrassment is to ask you right now to get out a piece of paper.

Next, I ask you to please fill in your idea of a very handsome, very cool guy who's dynamite.

(Leave yourself plenty of room for this description.)

This way my novel can't become too self-involved, since *you've* just described the hero.

One thing more.

Leah.

Leah has a lot to do with it—with this novel, my image, and all of it.

She has movie-star looks, the poise of a third-term president's daughter, dean's-list brains, and the sweet sensitivity of *Mozart 40*.

If you don't know what *Mozart 40* sounds like, stop in at your nearest record store and ask to hear it. I don't know much about classical music, and I know less about Mozart, but *Mozart 40* is a fluke in my life I'm not sorry about.

I'm not going to tell you the color of Leah's hair, because other girls have hair that color. Ditto, the color of her eyes. Ditto, her measurements. There is no sense in describing Leah in those ordinary terms. You would only try to conjure up the way Leah looks, and you'd be way, way off at best.

She is the twelve most beautiful words in the English language, which are reported to be:

> *cellar door*
> *dawn*
> *hush*
> *lullaby*
> *murmuring*
> *tranquil*
> *mist*

luminous
chimes
golden
melody
merit raise

All right—I don't know how "cellar door" and "merit raise" got on the list, either; I didn't make up the list.

But I think you appreciate, by now, what I mean about Leah.

We started going steady the first day I talked with Doomed.

Two

"Stein," I said, "our basketball team could really use a star as tall as you are."

I thought the "star" idea might appeal to him.

"I don't have star quality," Doomed answered.

"How do you know that? Have you ever tried being the star of something?"

"I don't go that route," said Doomed.

"What route do you go?" I asked.

"I'm *not* a jock."

"Stein," I said, "have you ever heard of Hank Greenberg, Sandy Koufax, or Mark Spitz?"

"Two were baseball players, one was a swimmer. So what?"

"So you should think about it a little more. Anyone can be a jock if he makes up his mind to be one."

"I don't get it," Stein said. "What do Greenberg, Koufax, and Spitz have to do with me?"

"Well, they're also of the Jewish persuasion," I said. "That fact shouldn't discourage anyone from going out for sports." (It was my grandfather who'd planted the idea in my head that there weren't many members of the Jewish persuasion who were keen on sports.)

Stein just looked through me for a moment. Then he said, "I'm not of any persuasion, except maybe the isolationist persuasion."

"No man is an island, Stein," I said.

"No man is the whole world, either, Bennett."

Doomed had my number, in a way, I guess. I suppose I gave the impression I thought I was the whole salami, despite the fact I live with a fifty-seven-year-old relative who never lets me forget that what I have won't last, and what I want isn't feasible. (We'll come to my mother later. She's always supportive, but then my mother is as kind as my grandfather is skeptical.)

This conversation with Doomed was taking place as we walked from homeroom to English. We were studying Alfred, Lord Tennyson's poem *In Memoriam* that week. The poem was a tribute to his friend, Arthur Hallam, who died suddenly of influenza when he was just twenty-two.

I said something to Doomed then about trying to make friends with him, and then I said, "Well I guess we'll never be known as Tennyson and Hallam, will we, Stein?"

Stein said, "Croak and find out, why don't you?"

How hostile can you get?

I repeated this conversation to Leah and her twin sister, Sophie, that night when I went over to the Penningtons'. We were sitting around in the rumpus room, which is the Penningtons' basement. We were drinking Cokes and listening to a new record album. Sophie was reading a biography of Sigmund Freud.

I have to explain about Sophie Pennington.

She's not at all like Leah. She says the reason is that she and Leah are dizygotic twins. If there's a four- or five-syllable way of explaining something, that's the way Sophie will put it to you. Dizygotic twins is just another way of describing fraternal twins, which means twins who don't have identical sets of genes.

Sophie is as different from Leah as night from day. You can start with her eyes, which are brown —Leah's aren't—and her eyesight, which is very bad—Leah's is excellent. You usually see Sophie wearing dark glasses. This is so no one will guess how thick her lenses are. For a long time the Penningtons wouldn't buy prescription dark glasses for her. Sophie began tinting her lenses herself with felt-tipped pens. Finally the Penningtons agreed to buy her a pair of prescription dark glasses, if she would promise not to wear them all the time. She's only supposed to wear them for things like football games, swimming at the beach, et cetera. She always wears them.

She's much taller and thinner than Leah, too. She has this very erect posture, and there's something almost militant about her manner. She's an extreme know-it-all—a foremost authority on every subject—and her ambition is to be a psychoanalyst. She got that idea from watching a television show that featured a shrink. But we like to kid her by saying she got the idea from Lucy in the "Peanuts" comic strip. Now and then Lucy sets herself up in business and gives psychiatric advice for seven cents. Our nickname for Sophie is "Doc."

This bossy beanpole in dark glasses, sounding off about everybody's complexes—that's half the picture. The other half falls into the "Physician, heal thyself" department—there is something very sick about Sophie's taste in boyfriends. My grandfather would describe them as "weak sisters." You'll get the idea as the novel progresses.

Anyway, that night in the Penningtons' rumpus room, after I finished telling them about my conversation with Doomed, Sophie got up abruptly and tipped her Coke bottle to her mouth to finish it off. Then she walked across the room toward the case of Cokes, as though she were going to return the empty bottle to it. When she passed me, she held the bottle upside down over my head, so the last few sticky drops hit my newly-washed hair.

I didn't say anything. You learn not to. I didn't move. I just let the gooey stuff dribble down to my ears, which were slowly turning red with anger.

Leah said, "That was a crude thing to do, Sophie!"

Sophie stuck the empty bottle in the case of Cokes. "It was a dramatization," she said.

"Of what?" Leah asked.

"Of exactly what you said—crudeness. So Alan can develop empathy for people like Duncan Stein."

I had my handkerchief out wiping off my ears and hair. "The whole point of my story was that I was trying to be very sympathetic with Duncan Stein."

"I said empathy," Sophie answered. "Not sympathy. There's a difference."

"He was trying to include Duncan Stein in things," Leah said. "What's wrong with that?"

"The way he did it," Sophie said. "Alan's the type who'd start off a conversation by mentioning Sidney Poitier or Martin Luther King if he was talking with a black."

She was exactly right, but I couldn't see anything wrong with that.

"What's wrong with that?" Leah said.

"You don't include somebody by right away

16

alluding to their major difference from you," said Sophie. "That's really crude."

"I don't even understand what you're talking about," Leah said.

I said I didn't either.

"Put it this way then," Sophie said. "Suppose I knew what I know about Alan, and I'd just met him for the first time. Okay?"

"Okay," we agreed.

"Okay," Sophie said. "Then suppose I started off the conversation by saying I'd like him to be my friend, because I had other friends whose fathers had deserted their mothers before they were born, too."

"SOPHIE!" Leah protested. "Oh, *Sophie*," she moaned.

"Did I make my point?" Sophie asked.

That's just an example of how Sophie makes her points.

After Sophie left the rumpus room, Leah tried to do everything to belittle Sophie, working on the theory that if she could do that, she could take the sting out of Sophie's remark.

Leah tried to get me to imagine the future, with Sophie listening to someone's troubles, as someone lay stretched out on her analytic couch.

"You see, Dr. Pennington," Leah imitated a distraught patient, "I can't get over my unhappy childhood. I was beaten black-and-blue by my father, and my mother was a drunk."

Then Leah became Sophie, the psychoanalyst. She did a pantomime of Sophie getting up, crossing to the couch, lifting the couch, and spilling her patient onto the floor.

"That's a dramatization of how you'll end up if you don't pull yourself together," Leah said, imitating Sophie's brusque tones.

Leah laughed hard then, hoping her laughter would have a contagious effect, and I'd pass by the whole matter.

But I'll tell you something about a situation like that: it's hard to let go of it.

I don't mean the hurt or the shock of Sophie's remark about my father. I've pretty much dealt with all that. What I mean is: Here was my opportunity to get a little extra well-deserved sympathy from someone great like Leah, with whom I'd wanted to go steady since the day we met.

I was almost grateful to Sophie, after the initial trauma.

We all have our little roles to play. We all exercise our emotions now and then. The way I did it that night was to imagine just how Sophie's remark would have affected me, if I *hadn't* ever gotten over the fact that my father had walked out on us back in the year one.

My face was a mixture of good sport trying to laugh along with Leah, and sad kid punched in the gut with an unhappy memory.

I clutched my hands together so tight my knuckles cracked, and then I pretended to be suddenly mortified at this show of raw nerves—I thrust my hands self-consciously behind my back.

Leah's face was beclouded with gentle concern for me. She sat down on the hassock in front of my chair and said, "Oh, *Alan*."

"I'll make it," I said solemnly, sniffing out a little smile. Okay. Corny. But haven't *you* ever pulled your own little scenes?

The next thing I knew Leah's arms were around me.

"I'm your girl, Alan," Leah said. "From now on, I'm your girl."

"Don't go steady with me just because you're sorry for me," I said.

"That's not why," she said.

"Then why?" I whispered back.

The rest of the scene is too personal. The result was that Leah and I were going steady.

I'll close this chapter with a sermon. I'll call it that before you do.

The thing is: I'm not going to describe in detail the very personal things that take place between me and Leah. I'm not writing this book for a bunch of voyeurs. I'm tired of books written for voyeurs. Go out and get your own experience, any of you voyeurs who happen to be reading this. It's a story about people and how their minds work, not a story about how their bodies work. Most people's bodies work pretty much the same way, and the clothes on their bodies come off in pretty much the same way. What's fascinating about people is, no one thinks or acts the same way. I am writing about the why of people.

For suspense, I'll tell you that the next chapter concerns an inside look at Lushing Brook.

Three

My mother makes a career of welcoming new families to Cayuta.

She works for Finger Lakes Friends as a hostess. When a new family moves into town, my mother calls on them with a big basket filled with gifts from local merchants.

She didn't call at Lushing Brook as promptly as she usually calls on newcomers. There were a lot of hard feelings in Cayuta when the people learned our city was going to become a haven for alcoholics who wanted to be rehabilitated. I guess everyone pictured a bunch of drunks staggering into town, falling down in the gutters, and sleeping in doorways. It took some time for the facts to penetrate. In the first place, very few candidates for Lushing Brook were average drunks; Lushing Brook was expensive. In the second place, none of them would even be seen in town. A limousine from Lushing Brook would meet the train or plane in nearby Syracuse and take the alkies straight to Lushing Brook. At Lushing Brook, there would be every facility, including an indoor screening room for movies, an indoor swimming pool, and several recreation rooms.

Finally my mother's clearance came through from F.L.F., and she scheduled her call for a Monday afternoon in late September. This was hard on me, because I usually helped her out.

At school, Monday afternoon was always reserved for football practice. In Coach Luther's eyes, it was The Most Important Practice Period of the Week. (Speaking of lushing, it wasn't an unlikely description of Coach Luther's weekends.)

At noon, I cornered him as he was coming out of the school cafeteria.

"What's your excuse, Bennett?" he asked when I told him I couldn't show up for practice.

His eyes were bloodshot, and his face was that ruddy color most people acquire outdoors in the sun or wind, instead of indoors in front of a Scotch bottle.

"I have to go to the dentist," I said. I couldn't say that I had to help my mother.

"You know damn well Monday is The Most Important Practice Period of the Week!" he barked back at me.

About fifteen years ago the name Lucius Luther was famous. He used to be a pro halfback with the Jaguars. Before that, he was a college hero. Before that, a high-school hero.

So much for ex-sports-heroes.

I felt sorry for him. Sometimes when he'd shoot his mouth off at us, I'd sense these strong vibrations that had to do with the fact he wasn't a young man anymore and we *were* young, and what he was beefed up about was what had become of him: he was this flunky coach in a nothing Upstate New York high school.

The only thing he really had going for him, until last summer, was this great-looking wife. No matter how badly he lost his temper or made a fool of himself, shouting about some little minor incident, there was this beautiful blonde picking him up every day after school in their little triumph convertible. You could always say, "Yeah, he's a foul-up, but he must be doing something right to have her."

Then she got it one night when he drove the Triumph into a tree. He didn't seem to do anything right after that, and that noon I had to deal with him.

I said, "Coach, I have an emergency tooth." Whatever I said to him always came out clumsily because I was afraid of him. Sometimes he'd cuff you across the back of the head; most of the time he'd yell some insult in your ear.

"You—stupid—" he said back to me, not finishing the sentence, walking away from me.

He could have been this neat guy, too. He could have been good-looking, if he hadn't let himself go to pot. Sometimes there was a trace of what he must have been like when he was younger—in his smile, or tone of voice—just a small sampling, and you could picture him when he used to be a winner.

Now he was just this slob, going gradually to fat, cantankerous and trigger-tempered, with coffee stains on his trousers and buttons off his sports coat.

I was telling my mother about him in the car, on the way to Lushing Brook.

"Poor *people*," my mother said. She was always saying that whenever she heard a pathetic story.

"What about his poor wife?" I muttered. "If he hadn't had a load on that night last summer, she'd still be alive."

"Just imagine having to live with that knowledge, Alan," my mother answered. (I liked her for being honest, anyway. Once I referred to the accident in front of my grandfather, and he said, "We have no proof of that, Alan, and you are never to indict the coach again!")

I told my mother: "He doesn't seem to live with it. He seems to take it out on everyone else."

"You should have known Lucius when he was your age, Alan," my mother said. "He had everything going for him, the way you do now."

"I'm going steady with Leah—did I tell you that, Mom?"

"A few hundred times," my mother said. "You used to tell me you'd never tie yourself down to one girl, remember?"

"I was a kid then," I said. "That's kid talk. The only ones who aren't going steady at school are the losers, the real losers."

"You use the words 'winner' and 'loser' too freely, Alan," she said, "I don't like it."

"It's a fact of life, though. There are the winners, and there are the losers. Of course," I added generously, "there are some in-betweens."

"But you don't always have such control over your life," my mother said. "There are things that can change a winner or an in-between into a loser, overnight. Something a doctor tells you, or sudden bad news someone tells you over the telephone—any number of things."

She didn't say "someone walking out on you"; she didn't have to. I got the point, and I felt badly, because I didn't want her to ever think she was a loser in my eyes. She was anything but; she was what kept me together, and everything she'd done for me she'd done by herself.

I said, "I don't count what other people do to you, or even what Fate does to you. I count what you do to yourself and your own life."

"Unfortunately," my mother said, "or fortunately, we don't live lives that are uninfluenced by other people and Fate. That's all part of life, and it's the biggest part."

We were at Lushing Brook then, and my mother turned onto the winding road leading up to the main building.

"I hope Mrs. Stein expects us," I said.

"Yes, of course. I called her."

"I hope I don't have to talk to Doomed while you're selling her on Cayuta."

"Why do you insist on calling that boy 'Doomed'?"

"Never mind," I said. "We'd just have to go into the winner-loser thing all over again."

This woman was waiting for us in the driveway.

She was a very beautiful woman, and immediately I wondered if she were some glamorous movie star who had come to Lushing Brook to dry out. I had never seen anyone quite like her. Leah is beautiful, too, but she is not yet a woman —she's often shy, and sometimes chews gum. I could never imagine this woman chewing gum. I could imagine this woman greeting royalty, or fending off photographers, or waiting in the middle of some bridge on a foggy night for a rendezvous with a famous man.

She said, "Just park anywhere. Hi!"

I got out of the car first and tried to hang back until my mother got out on her side. But the woman came straight for me, with this long black hair spilling past her shoulders, and these bright green eyes trying to look straight into my eyes. I looked down at the ground. I'm not one of these eye-to-eye people until I get to know someone.

"You must be Alan," she said. "I'm Catherine."

"Hello, Catherine," I said, and I noticed my mother giving me a dirty look.

"Hello, *Mrs.* Stein," she said.

"Please call me Catherine," the woman said to my mother, but I knew my mother had used the "Mrs." for my benefit.

It had truly never dawned on me that this woman could be Doomed's mother.

All I can say is there was Instant Magic. For once, I didn't care how long my mother's visit took.

My feeling about Catherine Stein had nothing to do with my feeling for Leah. It was something else; it was very deep inside and unreachable. I was suddenly shy; I also became surprisingly awkward and dense.

Doomed was nowhere in sight. But his name entered the conversation several times.

My mother spread out all her stuff on this big table in the Steins' living room. She began explaining about the shopping center on the outskirts of Cayuta, the advantage of milk and egg deliveries from Dairyking—all the jazz she was paid to push.

I was staring out of this huge picture window facing the gardens, where a few people were walking and reading. I knew these people were probably the drunks. But I wasn't even particularly curious about them, as I might have been normally, because of Catherine Stein.

My English teacher always says it isn't enough to write that the day was fun or the night beautiful. You have to give examples. I'd like to be able to give some examples of why I felt this way.

How the hell do I know why I felt what I did? Some people are compelling, that's all. A talent scout might know what I mean. A talent scout just picks out someone on sight sometimes—someone who doesn't sing or dance or do anything; someone who's just there and COMPELLING.

"Thanks for trying to get Duncan interested in sports, Alan," she said to me, while my mother was digging in her basket for free tickets to something. "Nice try."

"Oh? Did he tell you?" I said.

"We had a good laugh at that one," she said, cutting me to the quick, because I never thought there was anything in the incident for Doomed or his family to laugh at.

She added, "Duncan would lead your team to sure defeat in a matter of minutes," and she laughed some more.

I tried to laugh, too, but it was obviously an inside joke.

"Duncan wants to be a newspaperman," Mrs. Stein said.

"Well, we have a school newspaper he could write for," I told her.

"So Dunc tells me. I think he wants to start his own newspaper."

"Why not?" I said politely. I felt sorry for her because she seemed to think it was a good idea. I don't think anyone read our school newspaper except faculty and the kids who wrote for it. I couldn't imagine one soul reading a newspaper Duncan Stein put out.

My mother broke in at this point: "I'd like to recommend Wilton Dry Cleaners. Here's a complimentary ticket for a suit and a dress—"

The only time I lost this special feeling about Catherine Stein was when she talked about Doomed. Somehow it was like the Mona Lisa suddenly looking down from her frame and launching into a discussion of the local Chevrolet dealer, the Avon lady, or the bowlegged boy who lived across the street from you.

I kept thinking: *She* gave birth to *that?*

There was even a picture of Doomed on a desk in a corner of the room. I felt really sorry for her when I saw it. It took a lot of guts to put that thing in a gold frame and stick it on your desk in plain view, and have to answer people by saying, "Yes, that's my son."

At another point when my mother was trying

to find the slip for the free pound cake from Kelly's Baked Goods, Mrs. Stein asked me if I played tennis.

My mother said, "Alan goes steady with the tennis champ at Cayuta High."

"Congratulations," Mrs. Stein smiled.

For some reason I felt as asinine as I did once, years ago, when our Boy-Scout troop did drills before a whole division of infantrymen from Camp Lawton. Kid stuff.

I felt like this little puke whose only claim to fame was he went with some local high-school girl who beat out the Moravia High School tennis champ.

I tried to improve my image by saying, "I'm not big in the world of sports, either. I'll probably be a novelist."

At the time, I didn't even know if she'd heard me.

She said the reason she asked was that she was going to put in a tennis court for her "guests," and she badly needed advice. She added, "Dunc's father isn't any better at sports than Dunc. You're right, Alan—Jews aren't great jocks."

My mother looked up, startled.

You could have heard a feather fall.

I said, "I never said anything like that. I said something like that, but I never said that people of the—that those of the Jewish persuasion couldn't play sports well. I . . ." And then I just ground to a stop.

Mrs. Stein giggled. *"That* was the expression," she said. "People of the Jewish persuasion. . . . Dunc tried to remember it for us."

My mother was blushing. She said, "Alan never told me about this conversation."

"We were just amused at the way he put it," Mrs. Stein told my mother. "People of the Jewish persuasion . . . it's cute." And she giggled again.

My mother said, "We've tried to bring Alan up to know that everyone is equal in God's eyes."

"Of course you have," Mrs. Stein said nicely. "We've tried to bring Dunc up appreciating the same thing."

My mother had the slip from Kelly's Baked Goods in her hand, but before she presented it, I cut in.

"If you want to know anything about tennis courts and equipment," I said, "get in touch with Lucius Luther, our coach at school."

Mrs. Stein wrote the name down on a piece of paper.

That was that until we left Lushing Brook. Mrs. Stein walked us out to the car. While my mother went around to get in on her side, Mrs. Stein looked at me, smiling, trying for the eye-to-eye thing again, and she said, "I've enjoyed meeting you, Alan."

"Same here," I managed.

"Tell Dunc to bring you home for dinner some night," she said. "I used to be a columnist for the old New York *Herald Tribune*. I always wanted to be a novelist, too."

I was so delighted that she'd heard my remark about wanting to be a novelist, that I lost my guard and stared straight into her eyes. "Thanks," I said. "Thanks."

"That's all right," she said. "We people of the Christian persuasion have to stick together." Then she winked and gave me a big smile.

Four

We are probably the only high school in the country that makes a big fuss over Columbus Day. Every year on Columbus Day, we hold the Discovery Dance. It's a tradition. Since our school isn't a very rah-rah institution with a lot of so-called school spirit, nobody questions why we suddenly come alive every October. Most of us are just grateful there's a day when we *do* go into action.

The point of the Discovery Dance is supposed to be to discover someone new to go out with for that evening. A few people make an effort to do just that, but they are mostly shy kids, who don't go steady, or date very much. Most of us attend the dance with the same person we go to everything else with. For example, it wouldn't have occurred to me to ask anyone but Leah. At Cayuta

High, most of us go two-by-two, the way the animals entered Noah's Ark.

Sophie Pennington is an exception, only because Sophie is forever changing partners. She goes steady with about six guys a year. If this makes her sound like Miss Popularity, it isn't the case. The truth is: Sophie creates her own luck— if you want to call it luck. She is not one to wait for something to happen to her, or to wait for someone to take her out. Sophie often does the asking herself. The fact that she's a senior and the boy might be a junior or a sophomore, doesn't stand in her way. She's not age-conscious. In a way, she's not conscious of anything: height, weight, color of eyes, et cetera.

This particular October afternoon, we were all sitting around in Murray's after school, discussing the Discovery Dance. Sophie had just told us she'd asked Norman Putnam.

"Norman Putnam!" I said. "He's only about fourteen years old!"

Sophie's dark glasses were always sliding forward on her nose.

She pushed them back in one of her usual abrupt gestures, and seemed to eye me with a patronizing tolerance. (I can never be sure exactly how Sophie is eyeing me, because I rarely see her eyes.)

"Norman Putnam," she said. "Now here's a case

34

of someone suffering the trauma of living under the same roof with an auctioneer father."

"Oh, Doc," Leah sighed, "spare us the analysis."

"And developing a psychoneurotic condition as a result," Sophie continued.

"Norman Putnam," I said, "is just a run-of-the-mill flapjaw."

"There's nothing run-of-the-mill about Norman Putnam's incessant talking," Sophie said. "He's suffering from a condition known as logorrhea."

"Is that diarrhea of the mouth?" I said, trying to be funny.

"Exactly, Alan," Sophie said. "Exactly. Here's a case of a boy who's competing with his father."

"Going, going, gone," Leah said, imitating Mr. Putnam.

Mr. Putnam always presided at local auctions. I saw him in action once at a cattle auction my grandfather took me to.

I have to admit, Sophie's theory was interesting. Her theories are often interesting, when they're not directed against you.

Nearly everyone Sophie dates becomes a "case." Sophie never says, "I like John Doe. He has blue eyes and dances fantastically." She'll say something like, "John Doe. Here's a case of someone suffering from—" and then she'll start in on the diagnosis.

Leah said, "What did you do, Sophie? Just go up to Norman Putnam and ask him to go to the Discovery Dance with you?"

"Sometimes you're really juvenile," Sophie answered.

"Well what did you do?" I asked.

"I bought some tickets and told him he could go with me, if he'd let *me* talk fifty percent of the time," Sophie said. "I wouldn't put myself up for grabs without some kind of understanding. What do you think I am?"

The question went unanswered.

There were others at the table with us, and the conversation turned to a discussion of whose house we could invade after the dance. The most important part of a dance is where you go afterward.

My house is always available, but always a last resort, because as available as it is, my grandfather is equally available in it. The "make yourself scarce" attitude other families are willing to assume to make a group of us relax in a home environment is not an attitude my grandfather comes by easily. He is a snoop and a meddler, and a flop as a host to teen-agers.

We were also discussing who had the darkest basement, or the most rooms to find some privacy in, or the best parents. Ideally, in this situation, the parents would be deaf, dumb, and immobilized by fatigue.

So here we were—a gang of us—sitting around in Murray's trying to figure out how best to make out after the Discovery Dance, when this little kid from grammar school appears on the scene with a stack of newspapers in his arms. He's selling them for ten cents apiece.

"What's the name of the newspaper?" I said when he came to our table.

He placed one of the newspapers on the table.

REMOTE

"Remote?" I laughed. *"Remote?"*

"I just sell them," the kid said. "I don't know anything about this paper."

Then my eye caught the quotation printed up in a corner above the masthead.

> *" 'Tis better to have loved and lost*
> *Than never to have loved at all."*

My old brain began clicking away. The first thing I remembered was the quotation. It was from that poem we'd just finished studying in English, the Tennyson one, *In Memoriam*.

This reminded me of walking from homeroom with Doomed that day, remarking that we'd never turn into another Tennyson and Hallam.

The next thing I remembered was Doomed's

mother telling me that he wanted to start his own underground newspaper.

By this time my curiosity was racing like a downhill skier, and I pushed the dime in front of my Coke at the kid, and grabbed the paper.

The entire front page of *REMOTE* featured this head-and-shoulders etching of a woman in a high-collared dress. Her features were sort of indistinct and blurred, as though the etching was very old. She was a young woman, unsmiling, and in my judgment definitely average-looking.

Above her photograph were the words: *REMOTE salutes. . . .* Underneath the picture, the words: BEATRICE PORTINARI. Then these sentences:

> *Beatrice Portinari was the love of Dante's life. She was Dante's inspiration, and he made her his guide through Paradise in the* Divina Commedia. *She never returned his love, but married another and died young.*

That was the entire front page.

Leah was looking over my shoulder. "What does it mean?" she asked.

"I don't have the slightest idea," I said.

"Turn the page," Sophie said. "What kind of a newspaper *is* this?"

I turned the page. Page two featured a story signed with the initials D.S. The title was "I

Never Even Knew Her Name." Next to the title was a crude drawing of two stars crossing each other.

We scanned the story. (It was written in the first person, too.) It was about sitting next to a redheaded girl on a bus ride from New York to Boston. The narrator described how he and the girl slept beside each other for a few hours, shared an orange, and then discussed a bouquet of withering anemones she was carrying. She told him there was a legend that anemones were created from the blood of the poet, Adonis, who was loved by Aphrodite. The narrator fell madly in love with her during the bus ride. When they reached Boston, he collected his luggage from the rear of the bus, and returned to ask her name. But instead, he caught one last glimpse of her as she disappeared into the crowd. The last sentence of the story read:

> *Now and then I buy a small bunch of anemones, not to help me remember her—I can never forget her—but just to have them for a while, as I had her beloved presence for so short a time.*

"Wow!" Leah said appreciatively. "Wow!"

I just groaned, and then I said, "You know who wrote this mush?"

"Who?" Leah asked.

"Doomed," I said. "The D.S. stands for Duncan Stein."

"Duncan Stein," Sophie said. "Here's a case of an outcast compensating for his lack of popularity by inventing a great love story."

"A great love story?" I said. "He gets on a bus, falls asleep, mooches half an orange off the girl next to him, has a brief conversation about some dying flowers, and then writes it up like he'd made out with her in the moonlight to the music of a thousand violins."

Leah chuckled. "And if her presence was so beloved," she said, "how come he got his luggage *before* he tried to find out her name?"

"Right!" I said, pleased that Leah hadn't really been taken in by Doomed's pathetic little tale. "And if her presence was so beloved, how come he slept through most of the bus ride?"

Sophie said, "Go on to the next page. This is a weirdo newspaper."

One of the guys sitting at the table with us said to let him out first, because he didn't have time to sit around looking at a lot of bilge water. A couple of the others left with him.

"*REMOTE* seems to have all the appeal Doomed has," I said. Then I turned my attention to page three.

REMOTE will accept a limited amount of want ads in every issue. These ads must be in the spirit of the sample ads below. Rates can be discussed with Duncan Stein, phone: 486-0243. Mr. Stein will not discuss business in person—only over the phone. The first ad in the sampling is genuine.

The first ad read:

WANTED

A date for the Discovery Dance. She must be redheaded. It will be our one and only date. After that evening, there will never be any communication between us again. For an interview, call Duncan Stein, 486-0243, any evening between 7 and 9.

"Do you believe it?" I hooted. "Do you be-*lieve* it!"

"He's bonkers," Leah said. "He's one hundred percent bonkers."

Sophie didn't even say, "Here's a case of—" She just sat there with her mouth hanging open.

Here's a few of the other sample want ads:

WANTED

I will exchange photographs with girl willing to enter into brief correspondence with me. We will write each other with complete honesty, sharing all our secret thoughts. We will never meet. We will never speak to each other on the phone. After six letters have passed between us, we will end our relationship. Box A.

WANTED

I would like to go for a walk with a boy for one hour. We will choose a love poem to discuss during the walk. We will not touch during the walk. We will discuss nothing but the poem agreed on. At the end of the hour, we will never see each other again. Box B.

WANTED

Someone to send a rose to. I do not want to know anything about you but your name and address. I do not want to have any other communication with you once the rose is sent. I will write a personal message on card accompanying rose, but do not acknowledge it. Box C.

"Bonkers!" Leah kept murmuring.

"Let's see the last page," Sophie said.

I said, "Oh, Doomed, Doomed, is *this* the route you go?" I turned to the last page, which was the back of the newspaper. This is what I saw:

EDITORIAL

Editorials, like love, should be short and meaningful.

Going steady is going stale. It is also an uninspiring condition. Nothing of permanent value in romantic literature was ever written about going steady.

The star-crossed lover is both heroic and worthy of universal attention. This newspaper will celebrate him/her, and reflect the joy of unrequited and ephemeral love.

"Well, Doc," I said to Sophie, "what do you make of it?"

"It's what I said it was," Sophie answered, "but it's a more advanced case than I'd realized."

"I don't think I could stand unrequited love," Leah said.

"You have nothing to worry about," I told her.

Sophie said, "If I hadn't already asked Norman Putnam to the Discovery Dance, I'd buy a red wig and answer that want ad myself." She took off her dark glasses and rubbed her eyes wearily. "This is very definitely a case for Dr. Freud," she said.

I thought of Doomed's mother. I'd thought about her a lot since meeting her. She'd slowly become a regular part of my fantasy life. But I promised myself then and there that I was going to stop thinking about her, before *I* went Doomed's route.

The funny thing is—I sort of understood what Doomed meant. He meant all the mystery and magic that builds in you, for example, when you've found someone who really stirs you, and maybe you've only had one conversation with her. I remember how it used to be when I'd see Leah in the halls at school, when I hardly knew her. If she didn't smile at me, I could crash into little pieces. When she did smile, I'd be high for hours and hours. There was nothing quite like that time in my life. It was unreal, and no doubt I was a little freaked out, but it was a very sweet sickness.

That's part of what Doomed meant, and in a way I hated him for reminding me of what it was like. (Sometimes I felt like Leah and I were this old married couple . . . *sometimes.*)

I tossed the newspaper aside. "What a horse's ass!" I said.

Then I held hands with Leah. That was really where it was at . . . wasn't it?

Five

Just before I reported for football practice, on the day of the Discovery Dance, I met Sophie Pennington on her way out of the girls' locker room.

"We're all going over to Norman Putnam's after the dance tonight," she said.

"I know," I said. "What color gown is Leah wearing? I have to get her corsage after practice."

"Get her gardenias," Sophie answered. "She likes to press her old corsages in *The Random House Dictionary of the English Language,* and gardenias have a romantic aroma."

Then Sophie pushed her dark glasses back on her nose and sighed. "And speaking of romantic aromas, there's this man with genuine star quality hanging out in the parking lot. I don't know who he's waiting for, but he is well worth seeing, if only one time, as a sort of eighth wonder."

"Maybe he's a new teacher," I said.

"His kind gets kept," Sophie said firmly. "We've been doing our cheers out in the lot because the gym's being decorated for tonight. So if we don't know any new cheers at the game Saturday, it's because El Unbelievable made us nervous."

I didn't pursue the conversation, because at this point I got a glimpse of Coach Luther, standing near the entrance to the boys' locker room. I looked around to see if anyone was behind me. No one was.

Coach Luther was staring ominously in my direction.

"I wonder what he wants," I said to Sophie.

"Sometimes I think you suffer from panphobia," she said.

"What's that?"

"A morbid fear of everything," she told me.

"Look at the expression on his face," I said. "He's steamed up about something."

Sophie gave me a little two-fingered salute and left.

I started walking toward the coach.

"Do you like to tell lies, Bennett?" he barked at me before I even reached him.

"What do you mean, Coach?"

"I mean that lie about having to go to the dentist, about having a 'tooth emergency.'"

I didn't go too close to him for fear he'd slug me. I said, "My teeth need a lot of work."

"They're going to need a lot of work if you ever lie to me again. I'll knock them down your throat."

I swallowed hard and shifted my weight from one foot to the other.

"Mrs. Stein called on me a while back. She told me you were out at her farm on a certain Monday afternoon."

"I had to help my mother," I admitted.

"Why did you lie about it?"

I shrugged.

"I suppose you think it reflects on your lousy reputation as Number One Hero if you have to help your mother, hah?"

"I didn't know how it'd go over with you," I said.

He grabbed me by the collar. "It'd go over better than a sniveling lie about your stupid teeth!" he said.

"I'm sorry," I said.

He let go of me. "I'm fed up with you kids and your stupid poses," he growled.

"Stupid" was one of his favorite words.

"What do you stupid half-pints imagine, that the world revolves around the silly stuff you're involved in?"

I stood there wondering how we were supposed to muster up ye old school spirit and win a game for the coach when he viewed everything we did as "silly stuff." Maybe that explained why we'd only won two out of six games that season.

"Shall I get into my practice clothes now?" I said.

"No!" he said. "You can help me with something now."

It turned out he was going to donate some old tennis nets to Lushing Brook until their new equipment arrived. He wanted me to help him carry them out to the car.

While he was loading me up with them, he kept muttering that it was my idea to get him involved in the project in the first place, and that all he needed was this kind of "shit detail." (Coaches aren't big in the world of putting things delicately.)

I was staggering under the weight of the nets as we went out the back door. The coach was carrying a few old rackets.

"This is very generous of you!" a voice called out as we walked to the parking lot, and that was when I got my first glimpse of El Unbelievable.

While I was letting this man's physical pulchritude ("beauty" is not a big enough word to describe El Unbelievable) register, I heard the coach mumbling, "This is Dr. Stein. Dr. Stein, this is Bennett."

"How do you do, Bennett?" The man beamed at me.

"My name is Alan," I said, trying to tell myself Doomed had an uncle or a cousin. "Alan Bennett," I said.

"Never mind the buildup," the coach told me. "Just load the stuff in the back seat."

Printed in tiny gold letters across the limousine door was:

RUSHING BROOK FARM

Dr. Stein said, "I'd have sent our driver, but he has the day off because he's working tonight."

The coach didn't answer. To fill the silence I said, "It's a neat car."

"We really appreciate this," Dr. Stein said to me, perceiving the fact that I was the only one responding to anything he had to say. "It's so nice of you to go to all this trouble."

The coach was just standing there scowling, never one to extend himself.

I said, "What are you a doctor of?"

"It's a Ph.D.," he answered, "not an M.D." Then he flashed me another of his dazzling smiles and added, "I was a psychology major."

I was dying to give Sophie this information. El Unbelievable was a soul mate for her. Believe me, in Cayuta, New York, at the high-school level, Sophie didn't run across too many people willing to discuss the workings of the mind.

I was also sort of mildly dying inside: of shock, because this individual was *Doomed's* flesh and blood; of resignation, because this individual had me beat by miles where looks and everything else was concerned; and of the bitter taste of a certain truth I had to admit—I was really mediocre, in the long run. I was small potatoes.

God knows, my grandfather and Coach Luther had tried often enough to communicate that idea to me, but I'd always kept my ego intact. Before I met El Unbelievable, I'd never really realized what a long way I had to go.

"Tell Duncan to bring you out to the farm for dinner some evening, Alan," he said after I stuffed the nets in the back seat of the limousine.

They must have lousy dinner hours, I thought, since both of Doomed's parents tossed that at me without even knowing anything about me. They probably couldn't stand being alone with Doomed—they'd most likely adopted him from some awful orphanage in the first place.

Then the doctor drove off, and I was left with Coach Luther. He was standing there watching the limousine speed away, with a thoughtful expression on his face, as though he was thinking the same thing I'd been thinking.

"Genetics is a great mystery, really," I said. "And I don't think we know all there is to know on the subject."

"Suit up and mind your own business," he told me.

Nice, I thought as I walked away from him—nice, and good luck with your mouth. So much for a solid relationship between student and faculty.

That night at quarter to nine, I arrived at the Penningtons' carrying a small florist's box, wearing my best navy blue suit. The girls were still wearing evening gowns to dances, but the boys had stopped renting tuxes about three years ago, except for a prom.

Leah is a pleasure. When I presented her with the corsage, she danced around like she'd never seen a gardenia before. She pinned it to her wrist, the way the girls at C.H.S. were doing that year, and then she darted upstairs to show her mother.

Mr. Pennington was sitting in his armchair reading the newspaper, ignoring me and Norman Putnam, who was perched on the edge of the living-room sofa.

"I got Sophie a rose corsage," Norman said, "but there're thorns in it and she's upstairs trying to fix them so they don't stab her. You'd think a florist would do something about thorns if he's selling rose corsages, wouldn't you, but old man Lettermen is a crook, anyway. My father auctioned off some antiques for him and he still owes my father for the day's work. But people often forget to pay an auctioneer, which is why my mother tries to get him to demand payment before he begins the auction, only my father's too polite. That's his ruination—he's generous to a fault."

Mr. Pennington let out this long agonized sigh behind his newspaper.

I said, "Is this your first big dance?"

He started to rattle off another long monologue, but Sophie appeared then. "I'm ready," she said.

Mr. Pennington was going to drive us there. He put his newspaper down and said, "You're not wearing dark glasses to a dance, I hope."

"I'm just wearing them over. I'll change to my others when we get there," she lied.

"You look preposterous wearing dark glasses and a ball gown," Mr. Pennington said.

"I'm not your date," Sophie said, "and Norman likes the way I look, don't you, Norman?"

"Yes," Norman said. "I think it's mysterious, and I don't mind it much because you always wear them. I wouldn't know you without them, I don't think. No, I wouldn't. I always think of them as your trademark. I wish I had a trademark myself, since it sort of stamps you and—"

"Your mouth is your trademark, Norman," Sophie said.

I said, "I wonder who Doomed will show up with?"

"Where's Leah?" Mr. Pennington said.

"He won't show up with anyone, if you ask me," Sophie said.

"Who's Doomed?" Norman asked.

"I'm ready." Leah appeared.

"You both look very nice," Mr. Pennington said.

"I wish I had a gardenia," Sophie said.

"You look beautiful, Leah," I said.

"I would have brought you one if you'd told me," Norman said.

"Let's go," Mr. Pennington said.

The Discovery Dance was in full swing when we arrived. The C.H.S. Grand Awfuls were playing, as usual; as a little salute to Leah and me they played our song, one of their own originals, called "Lady, Be My Forever Lady."

There was really a big turnout for the dance, and even though it was raining, everyone looked great. All the girls had done their hair special, and all of them had their corsages fixed to their right wrists. You could see your face in the shines on the boys' shoes, and every one of them was wearing his best dark suit, and his own version of a neat tie and jazzy shirt to go with it.

I guess we'd all forgotten about Doomed for a while, but a little after ten thirty, a hush began to spread through the gym from the entrance all the way up to the bandstand. All you could hear was the music, and even that seemed to soften.

"What's up?" I asked Leah.

"Look," she said. "Down near the stage line."

I saw Doomed first, because he's so tall.

He wasn't just wearing a tux—that would have been unusual enough. He was wearing tails. In his buttonhole there was a red carnation. He looked like someone who'd just come from his own wedding. He was just standing there watching everyone with a slight smile tipping his lips, as though he were someone's father looking in on the kiddie dance.

"That's Gwendolyn Graney with him!" Leah said as we danced nearer.

"Who's she?"

"A freshman," Leah said. "Little Gwendolyn Graney."

She *was* little, too, not much over five feet two. She had bright red curly hair and a lot of freckles on her face and shoulders and wrists. She was wearing a black net gown that looked ridiculous on her, because she had no shape and was nearly as skinny as Doomed.

"What's she carrying?" Leah asked.

"Flowers."

She was carrying a small bouquet of these strange looking purple and red flowers, with black button centers.

"What kind of weeds are they?" I asked.

"Anemones," Leah answered. "I'll bet they're anemones."

"They look like they could use some water," I said.

"A redheaded girl with anemones," Leah said,

"just as he described in his story.*"

"Corn-*ny!*" I groaned.

Leah didn't say anything then. She just kept staring at Doomed and Gwendolyn Graney.

The music stopped momentarily, and Leah sidled across to Sophie and Norman Putnam. I followed, shaking my head with disbelief, and repeating, "Corn-*ny!*"

Norman said, "Not even a corsage. Even if I didn't get Sophie a gardenia like she wanted, I knew enough to get a *corsage* for her. I wouldn't show up with a bunch of cut flowers for a girl to have to carry all the way through a dance."

"I don't think Gwendolyn Graney's ever had a date before tonight," Leah said.

"And she had to answer a want ad to get this one," Sophie said.

Norman said, "Even though *you* bought the tickets and asked *me,* you're better off than someone who has to go through classifieds to find a date for the evening, if you ask me."

"Which I didn't," Sophie told him, "so pipe down. This is very interesting."

Then the music began again, a slow number. Doomed gave a slight bow in Gwendolyn Graney's direction and then took her in his arms to dance. She held the flowers in the hand which rested on his shoulder (it was a long reach for her) and Doomed looked down into her eyes as though she'd hypnotized him.

Gwendolyn Graney looked away, at first. She looked around the room at everyone (nearly everyone was staring at them) and a deep red color began to cover her freckles all the way down to her shoulder bones.

Then Doomed said something to her, and she looked back at him.

Doomed kept talking softly to her, and she kept looking at him, and after a while it was clear that *Doomed* was hypnotizing *her*, not the other way around. She began to relax. They began to behave as though they were the only dancers on the floor. For several long moments, they *were* the only ones dancing.

"This is boring," I finally said to Leah. "Let's go get some punch."

Leah said, "What is poor Gwendolyn Graney going to do after tonight?"

"What do you mean?" I said.

"I mean he's never going to see her again. His want ad said so. They have just this one night."

Norman Putnam said, "What's stopping him from calling her up again, if he wants to? All he has to do is call her up again, or walk up to her at school, for Pete's sake. I just don't see what's—"

"Pipe down, Norman," Sophie said. "He made it quite clear that he has no intention of seeing her after tonight. It was printed in the newspaper in black and white for all to see!"

"I still don't—" Norman began.

"You wouldn't," Sophie said. "You just wouldn't get it."

"It's all an act," I said. "Are we supposed to take it seriously?"

"It's an interesting act, is the point," Sophie said. "Why should we take a lot of dull reality seriously, when we've got an interesting act?"

"Poor Gwendolyn Graney!" Leah said. "I can see she's falling for him."

"For *Doomed?*" I said.

"Oh, this is awful," Leah said, ignoring my remark "This is so tragic."

"Let's go get some punch!" I said.

"Wait," Leah said. "I want to watch some more."

Everyone kept watching Doomed and Gwendolyn Graney. At first, only the girls seemed that interested, but ultimately the boys worked up an interest, too, since it seemed the only way to hold a conversation with the girls. There was speculation that Doomed was falling just as hard for Gwendolyn Graney as she was for him, and more speculation that the two of them would be going steady by morning.

But amidst all that speculation was the idea that Doomed had really meant what he'd said in his ad, and that regardless of how either one felt, he would stick to it.

There were even rumors that Doomed didn't have long to live, which was the reason he wouldn't get involved, and that Doomed had gigantic insanity somewhere in his family, which was the reason he couldn't get involved.

By midnight the entire Discovery Dance pivoted around Doomed and Gwendolyn Graney.

Doomed never took his eyes off her. Doomed wouldn't let anyone else cut in. (A few characters tried to, just to get Gwendolyn's version of the relationship.) Doomed managed to inspire a wide range of expressions on her poor, pinched face: utter happiness; wistfulness; solemnity; amusement; and tenderness.

Hands down, they were the stars of the evening. Just before the Grand Awfuls played their last set, Norman Putnam, pushed halfway across the room by Sophie, approached them to ask if they'd care to accompany the gang to his house after the dance. He came away shaking his head from side to side.

"They refused?" Sophie said in an awed tone, pushing her dark glasses back on her nose.

"He refused for them," said Norman. "He was very polite about it, but he said they intended to have a quiet supper alone together, with a little soft music in the background."

"That is the most interesting delusion I've come across since reading up on galeanthropy," said Sophie. "A quiet supper alone together at this hour!"

"What's galeanthropy?" I asked.

Sophie said, "It's the delusion that you've been turned into a cat."

"Did you tell him there's nothing open at this hour?" Leah asked Norman.

"Yes, I did," said Norman. "And he said they were going back to Rushing Brook."

"I *don't* believe it!" Sophie said. "I don't *believe* it!"

But it was true, all right. We found that out while we were all huddled together outside in the parking lot, waiting for Mr. Putnam to arrive. Leah and Sophie, like a lot of girls at C.H.S., were not allowed to ride in boys' cars late at night— and anyway, none of us had our own cars yet. It was Mr. Putnam's turn to do the driving.

Just as Mr. Putnam chugged up in his years-old station wagon, the Rushing Brook limousine arrived on the scene.

We all stood there getting wet, with our mouths hanging open.

Out of the limousine, in full uniform, stepped this cool chauffeur carrying an open umbrella. He marched himself up to the side door of the gymnasium. Returning under the umbrella, while the chauffeur held it over their heads, were Doomed and Gwendolyn Graney. Gwendolyn was still carrying the anemones.

The chauffeur opened the door of the back seat

for them. Doomed gave another of his little bows, reached for her hand, and helped her to the long limousine.

"Well, what are you youngsters waiting for?" Mr. Putnam shouted at us. "Pile in! Party, party!"

I made my own little bow to Leah, but she didn't even notice. She was watching the limousine speed away.

Six

For years the parents and teachers have complained about the Discovery Dance, because Columbus Day usually falls on a weekday. They have tried to have the dance pushed forward to a Friday or Saturday night. They claim it's in the interest of the students, who are supposed to fall apart the next day from lack of sleep. We suspect it's in their own interests. Therefore, we're all extra careful about getting to school on time the next day, and being super-alert in classes.

Because of this, I said, "Can't it wait?" when my mother announced at breakfast the next morning that she wanted to talk to me for a moment.

The mailman had just come by, and my mother placed a letter in front of my cereal bowl.

"I think you should read this now, and think it over during the day," she said.

The letter was from my father.

Dear Alice,

I know it's been a long time, far too long since I inquired about you and Alan.

Pam and I have done a lot of soul-searching. We've decided to depend on your sense of fair play in making this request. I know we haven't played fairly with you, but we haven't been at all proud of ourselves for that, and we've been unhappy because of it.

The thing is, I'd like to make my son's acquaintance. I don't expect to be able to pick up the father/son thing after all these years. I'm not a complete fool.

But I'd like to see Alan. I think it might be an important step for him to take, too. He's my only child, and I'm his only father. For that reason alone, it's important—whether he likes me or not.

It would be ideal if he could come to New York for a few days during his Christmas vacation. Please let me know what you and Alan think of the idea.

Sincerely,
Ken

I handed the letter back to my mother. "Is Pam the broad he ran off with?"

"Pam's his wife now, Alan."

"But she *is* the broad he ran off with?"

"Yes."

"No," I said. "Absolutely not."

"Give it some thought, Alan. Don't be so quick in your answer."

"You'd let me go visit him, with *her* there?"

"She has nothing to do with anything, anymore," my mother answered.

"As far as I'm concerned, she does."

"Think about it, dear."

"What's to think about?" I said. "He's a stranger and so's his broad."

"I won't answer the letter right away," my mother said.

"As far as I'm concerned, the answer is no."

My grandfather was already down at the store, so we didn't get his words of wisdom on the subject at that point. I couldn't wait until he feasted his eyes on that little letter!

I finished my cereal and didn't refer to the letter again. I put it out of my mind. I concentrated on school, and Leah, and memories of the night before: the dance, and afterward at Norman Putnam's.

Leah always came through. There were a lot of girls who just kept babbling on about Doomed and Gwendolyn Graney, when we got to the Putnams'. Even some of the boys got stuck on that subject. But Leah sensed my impatience and pulled out of it. We had a good time. She even agreed with me that the whole stunt was childish.

So I woke up in a neat mood that morning. I was determined not to let that letter get to me. I told myself that someday I'd write about it, *use* the experience, the way our English teacher told us to *use* life when we wrote. I packed up my book bag, whistling, and I gave my mother an extra-special hard hug.

Then I headed off to catch the bus.

I knew something was wrong with my head when I took the East Lake bus, instead of the regular one that takes me to Cayuta High every morning.

When I finally got off the bus, I was way up the lake. There's nothing there but farms and dirt roads.

I was aware that I was letting everyone at school down by skipping classes the day after the Discovery Dance, but I didn't particularly care.

So he was still with Pam, after sixteen years!

I'd never known her name. I knew that my father married my mother on the rebound from Pam. Then after my mother was pregnant (before I was even born!) Pam wagged her little finger at my father, and off he went with her.

El Reliable, as Sophie might say. About as reliable as a snowball in August.

I was walking along a dirt road thinking bitter thoughts—indulging myself, my grandfather would say.

It was a sunny morning and I was dressed too warmly. I took off my coat and slung it over my shoulder. After I'd walked about a mile, I went down to the edge of the lake and flopped down by a tree. I put my coat under my head, stretched out so the sun hit my face, and pretended I was a millionaire off at a swanky resort, resting up after a big night.

Then I began to enlarge on my fantasy. I'd become a millionaire by writing a best seller. It was about a man who'd run off with another woman when his wife was pregnant. Then the other woman ran off on him after sixteen years. I called it *Ditched*. With all the money I made from it, I bought my mother a new house and clothes and a long fancy sports car, and Leah and I got married and traveled all over Europe. My grandfather was in the fantasy too, admonishing us that none of it would last.

I'd only had a few hours' sleep the night before, and I just dozed off in the midst of my fantasy.

It was noon when I woke up. I'd indulged myself enough. I walked back up the dirt road and decided to head for the bus and return to school. Everyone was on lunch hour now. I'd just slip back and use the old "tooth emergency" excuse.

Then in the distance, I saw a familiar object headed in my direction. There's only one black limousine like that in all of Cayuta.

I ducked into a bush. For all I knew it was

Doomed, getting a late start for school, after his late-supper-to-soft-music of the night before. I realized I was just down the road from Lushing Brook. I don't know what had made me head for those parts.

When the limousine passed me, I saw Dr. Stein behind the wheel. He was by himself. El Unbelievable in all his glory.

I got a great idea. I would go to Lushing Brook and call a taxi. I had money left over from last night, plus lunch money (I wasn't hungry). I would call my mother, in case the school had called to ask where I was. My mother is a very understanding person. I'd just tell her I was a little upset by the letter, and I'd taken some time off from school to do some thinking.

Of course, Catherine Stein was part of it. I wanted to see her again. I wanted to, and I didn't want to. I wanted to because I felt some peculiar pull toward her—maybe way in the back of my mind it was why I had gone up to the lake in the first place. But I didn't want to because I was afraid I might come off like some kind of dummy. Possibly, I wouldn't even know how to make conversation with her while I waited for the taxi. Possibly, I'd just be interrupting her at something, and she'd be irritated at the intrusion.

I had mixed feelings and weak knees, but I went ahead anyway.

No one saw me approach Lushing Brook. Oh,

maybe some drunks drying out in there saw me as they looked out of their windows, but Catherine Stein didn't see me . . . and neither did Coach Luther.

I saw his car parked in the driveway as I walked toward the house. He drives that same blue triumph he drove into the tree last summer. There are still dents in the body, and like the coach himself, it's in seedy condition.

So I knew he was there, and that's when I began to lose my nerve and sneak around. I had almost decided to head away, and walk back to where the bus had left me off, down the road. Then I heard their voices.

They were back in the area where the tennis court was going to be. There are trees and shrubbery all around Lushing Brook, so it was easy to see them without being seen.

I figured the coach had come out on his lunch hour.

They were laughing an awful lot. For the coach, that's already erratic behavior, as Sophie would put it. They were talking too, but not in loud voices. They didn't have to talk in loud voices. They were standing very close together.

You could say that it was a perfectly innocent scene. She was carrying one of those clipboards with yellow paper attached to it, and a pencil. He was pointing to the ground and she was making notations. Okay. He was helping her. El Unbelievable didn't look like the type who cared much about laying out a tennis court. So you could say the coach was there for that purpose . . . out of the kindness of his heart . . . except Lucius Luther isn't known for his kindness or his heart.

He is also not known for his grooming, except negatively. That noon he looked like an ad for men's clothing. He had on this white V-necked tennis sweater (spotless from my vantage point), charcoal-gray flannel slacks, and newly shined loafers. He was even holding his stomach in.

She was in slacks and a sweater, with a bright red scarf holding back her long black hair. She doesn't need much description, because she is always beautiful.

The thing is: he touched her.

I know you're going to start hollering "So what!" and start imagining I'm this retard who makes ocean liners out of canoes—but that touch was definitely not in the canoe class.

Here's how it happened. They were standing there talking softly and chuckling, eye-to-eye, facing each other, and then he just lightly touched his fingers to her bare arm. She looked down at his fingers on her bare arm, and then she looked back up at him. He left his fingers there for a moment, and then he dropped them to his side.

During those slow seconds when he was touching her and they were looking into each other's eyes, their smiles vanished. They both had solemn looks.

After, he dropped his arm to his side, said something, and they laughed again—but not very hard this time. They also moved a little away from each other, as though it had just occurred to them they were standing awfully close for two people just interested in setting up a tennis court.

I heard her say, "Let's have some coffee!" It was as though she'd purposely raised her voice to change the tone of things.

"Great!" he shouted back at her, though he needn't have shouted. Then they went inside.

I made a shortcut through the fields, running. I just felt like running.

Seven

When I got back to school, lunch hour was almost over. I went into one of the phone booths just outside the cafeteria, to call my mother. It turned out she hadn't even known I'd missed my morning classes. I told her I'd had a delayed reaction to my so-called father's letter, and she said that was understandable, and that she'd write me an excuse.

While I was talking with her, I noticed a small mob of girls crowded around a table at the front of the cafeteria. Just beyond the mob, I caught a glimpse of Sophie, sitting by herself, reading.

"Are you okay now, Alan?" my mother asked.

"I'm fine," I said. "I took a walk up near the lake and cleared my head."

"You don't have to go visit him," she said.

"I know that," I told her. "I don't plan to."

After I hung up, I walked into the cafeteria. I had to stand on tiptoe to see who was the center of attention at the first table. It was Gwendolyn Graney.

I didn't see Leah in the mob, so I walked over to Sophie. She was reading *The New Dictionary of Psychology*. She barely glanced up at me, and kept reading as I talked to her.

"Where's Leah?" I asked.

"Am I my sister's keeper?" she answered.

"What's going on with Gwendolyn Graney?"

"Mass hysteria," she told me. "Guess what's she's carrying around? She's been carrying them around all morning."

"What?"

"Those old dead anemones," Sophie said. "She's been carrying around those old dead anemones."

I sat down opposite Sophie. "I missed classes this morning," I said.

"She fills me with misopsychia," Sophie continued, ignoring my remark.

"What's misopsychia?"

"A generalized disgust with life." She yawned. "It's listed here in my book after misopedia. Misopedia is a neurotic dislike of one's own children. This is not a simple world we live in. It's filled with pathology."

"I never heard of anyone disliking their own

children," I said. "Somebody might abandon his own child, or ignore his own child for a long time, but I never heard of anyone actually disliking his own child."

"Well, it's here in this book in black and white," Sophie said. "If it didn't exist, there wouldn't be a name for it."

"What's she carrying around those old dead flowers for?" I said.

Sophie said, "Stop pestering me. Leah's practicing cheers down in the gym."

I sauntered away nonchalantly, as though it really hadn't bothered me at all that she'd ignored my remark about missing school, and then ordered me to stop pestering her.

In about twenty years, when Sophie didn't have anyplace to go, including Leah's and my house, I'd recall a few instances like this one for her.

The afternoon bell rang while I was putting my coat in my locker. I went off to English class suffering from my own case of misopsychia.

Doomed sat a few seats away from me in English.

We were still studying the Victorian poets. When our teacher asked if any of us had a favorite poem, Doomed's hand shot up in the air.

"Which one is it?" Mrs. Tompkins asked him.

" 'Love Song,' " Doomed answered, "by Arthur Symons."

"Do you want to read it to us?" she asked.

"I know it by heart," Doomed answered. Then he stood up and recited it.

> O woman of my love, I am walking with
>   you on the sand,
> And the moon's white on the sand, and the
>   foam's white in the sea;
> And I am thinking my own thoughts, and
>   your hand is on my hand,
> And your heart thinks by my side, and it's
>   not thinking of me.
> O woman of my love, the world is narrow
>   and wide,
> And I wonder which is the lonelier of us
>   two:
> You are thinking of one who is near to your
>   heart, and far from your side;
> I am thinking my own thoughts, and they
>   are all thoughts of you.

The girl behind me sighed very loud, and another girl clapped.

Mrs. Tompkins said, "And why do you like that poem so much, Duncan?"

Doomed said, "Because they both feel intense love but there is no way either one can express it. She is not with the man she loves, and he loves her but realizes she loves someone else. Suffering —that's what love is all about."

Mrs. Tompkins smiled slightly as though she

knew more than Doomed did about love. "Oh?" she said. "I thought love was about two people giving and taking together."

"That's not love," Doomed said. "That's a fifty-fifty arrangement."

"I see," Mrs. Tompkins said. "What do the rest of you think?"

The girl behind me said, "I think there's a difference between romantic love and fifty-fifty type love."

"I think," another girl said, "that fifty-fifty type love is for older people who want to get married."

Then everyone started talking about what they thought love was.

I didn't contribute. I listened to everyone, but I didn't feel like joining in. I was thinking about my father's letter again . . . and about the little scene I'd watched at Lushing Brook.

I kept telling myself that if you feel love, the way I felt about Leah, there wasn't a lot to talk about . . . and yet, what they were talking about had a lot to do with why my father just took off that way, and also, I suspected, with what the long look between Catherine Stein and Coach Luther meant. The closest I ever came to that kind of intense feeling was when I was first falling for Leah, but I knew that I was probably nowhere near to suffering, even then. It could be, I thought, that some people aren't cut out for that sort of emotion. I guess that in a way I viewed it as a terrible weakness, a flaw. After all, it was the sort of emotion that had left my mother without a husband, or a father to her child. I was the fifty-fifty type. Solid Sam.

"Well, Duncan," Mrs. Tompkins said when the bell finally rang, "you provided us all with a lot of food for thought."

As I was leaving, I noticed some of the girls hanging back to talk to Doomed.

I didn't see anything of Leah that afternoon. We kept missing each other in the halls between classes; after school I had football practice.

While I was suiting up, the fellow next to me said, "I'm going to catch hell because I left my jersey home."

Even for practice, the coach insisted we wear the green jersey shirts and the white pants. If one of us wasn't in green and white, he practically went ape with rage.

I said, "I'd rather miss practice altogether, Dave."

"I know it," Dave said, "but he knows I'm here. I'm trapped."

We all ran out on the field and stood in a row like buck privates shaping up before the top sergeant.

Then Coach Luther came striding out toward us, while we shivered in the afternoon breeze and waited for him to pick on someone for something.

He spotted Dave right away.

"Hey, clown!" he shouted at him. "Where's your green?"

Dave had on a navy blue jersey.

"I left it home, sir," he said. "I'm sorry."

"Don't forget it next time," said the Coach.

Don't forget it next time? I stood there, incredulous. I was waiting for the trick ending; there had to be one: a sudden barrage of obscenity, or a cuff across Dave's neck . . . something . . . but the coach was down at the other end of the line by then, talking with one of the quarterbacks.

"I wish he wouldn't leave me in suspense like this," Dave whispered to me. "I wish he'd just get my punishment over with."

Dave never heard another word about it though.

Afternoon practice that day was really weird. It was as though some benevolent form of life from outer space had temporarily taken over the coach's mind and spirit. He smiled at us more that afternoon than he'd smiled at us for three years and two months. He didn't stop calling us "stupid," and he still had the same old mean mouth, but his heart wasn't in it. It was like someone only a third as nasty as he is, impersonating him.

There was something else strange about him, too. He wasn't wearing his filthy old green-and-white jumpsuit. He was wearing one of his old green-and-white jumpsuits, all right, but it was clean.

He also had a new haircut. He also let us go by four thirty, instead of working us until it was dark out.

Back in the locker room, Dave remarked, "What's wrong with him?"

"I don't know," I said. But I had a sinking feeling that I did know.

When I got home, I expected my grandfather to go into one of his fits over my father's letter. It was on the table beside his armchair when I came in the door. He was reading the evening paper.

He's a big man with thick gray hair, the kind who wears a necktie until he goes to bed, and never rolls up his shirtsleeves. I don't think he's ever missed a Sunday of church or a Tuesday Rotary meeting down at the Cayuta Hotel. The pillar-of-the-community type.

I mumbled something about the mailman not caring what kind of trash he delivered to the door, and flopped down on the couch.

My grandfather lowered his newspaper. "Your mother tells me you don't want to go to New York."

"That's right," I said. "And I'm not going to change my mind."

"It's your decision," he said.

It struck me as interesting that suddenly something was *my* decision, with no interference from him.

I said, "Then we don't have to talk it into the ground." Actually, I wanted to talk about it. At least, I wanted him to talk about it. I expected him to blow up at my father, or show some kind of disapproval.

"We don't have to mention it again," he said, going back to his newspaper.

"I wouldn't visit him in New York if they were giving away million-dollar bills," I said.

"It's your decision," he repeated.

"What makes him think I give a damn about him, after all this time?" I said.

"I don't know," he said.

"I couldn't care less!" I said.

Silence from him.

The subject never came up during dinner, either. I picked at my food and made plans to go over to Leah's for the evening. I had an idea Leah would be the only one to talk with about it, but I knew I'd start off by telling her I didn't want to discuss it, and depend on her to coax it out of me.

I helped my mother with the dishes, and then I called the Penningtons'.

"I'll probably come over for a while," I said to Leah.

"Not tonight, Alan," she said. "Some of the girls are coming over."

"Since when?" I said.

"I'm allowed girlfriends, aren't I?" she said.

"Well, what are you all planning to do that other people can't join in?"

"It's a hen party," she said. "We're going to run ads in REMOTE, and we want to write them up."

"You're kidding!" I said.

"Just for fun," she said.

"It sounds pretty stupid to me."

"That's why it's a hen party," she said. "Certain people of the masculine sex don't have any sense of humor."

"I missed school this morning," I told her.

"I can't talk now, Alan," she said. "The girls are coming in a few minutes, and I have to help Sophie clean the rumpus room."

"I bet it's all Sophie's idea," I said.

"Was it a Browning poem or a Symons poem he read in your English class this afternoon?" Leah asked me.

"He didn't read it," I said. "He recited it. And how did you hear about that?"

"Everyone's been talking about it," she said.

"It was Symons," I said.

"Thanks a lot, Alan," Leah said. "See you tomorrow?"

Then I heard a click and a dial tone. She hadn't even waited for my answer.

I suppose that's part of love, too—taking someone for granted. But it didn't strike me as the best part, that night.

Eight

The last Saturday in October we were scheduled to play Moravia High School at two thirty.

On game day we always reported to the locker room by one thirty. We suited up and sat around, going over old plays, discussing what we knew about individual opponents (there was a real bone-breaker on the Moravia team named Leogrande), gossiping some, and climbing the ladder to peer out at the stadium from the high locker-room window.

For a while Dave and I sat by our lockers and talked about this Leogrande. Dave was frankly worried about his own nose getting it. He'd broken his nose once already, falling off the back end of a motorbike. He came from a family of big noses, anyway, and now his was even bigger than usual. He said it didn't bother him that much, but his girl would hate it if he turned out to have this gigantic nose just because he'd played football in high school.

I said something about looks not really counting, and he said that was easy enough for me to say—I had nothing to worry about.

"Do you think the coach is even slightly handsome?" I asked him.

He laughed and said he was as handsome as any chimpanzee.

"Still," I said, "he had a beautiful wife."

"He married her when he was very young," Dave said, "before he turned into a chimpanzee."

I agreed. I said I couldn't imagine any woman falling for the coach.

I sat there thinking about it, while Dave climbed the ladder to watch the crowd pour into the stadium.

Then I got this brainstorm. I didn't know why I hadn't ever thought of it before. The coach drank, and the Steins made a business out of curing drunks. That could explain everything, couldn't it? Couldn't Catherine Stein just be sorry for the coach, or interested in rehabilitating him?

I mulled that over for a while, and it seemed to fit. I even ran through the old touching-her-arm scene, and their subsequent long look, and it still fit. He was looking to her to save him from himself, and she was picking up on the message.

I was beginning to feel better. It wasn't any of my business what the coach or Catherine Stein did with their personal lives, but I liked things to make sense. I didn't like to think I was completely stupid about people. How was I ever going to write about people if I couldn't get through to the real facts?

Dave interrupted my thoughts with a four-letter word I'll spare you. He was on top of the ladder, looking out the window.

"What's wrong?" I shouted at him.

"The stadium's three-quarters full," he said, "and everyone's reading."

"Oh, sure," I said. "Football fans are known for their lust to learn."

"I'm not kidding, Alan," he said, climbing down from the ladder. "Doomed's got a bunch of kids selling that damn newspaper of his outside the gate, and everyone's reading it now."

I took his place at the top of the ladder and peered out at the crowd. Not everyone was reading, but about every fourth person's face was hidden behind a copy of REMOTE.

"It's the new issue," Dave said. "I bought a copy myself, on my way in."

"Why?" I said.

"What?"

"Why would you buy a copy of REMOTE?"

"I think my girl's got an ad in it somewhere," he said. "A lot of the girls were buying ads in it, didn't you hear?"

"I heard," I said, "but that wouldn't make me spend a dime for the rag." I took a last look at the stadium. Even on the Moravia side you could see heads buried behind that corny newspaper of Doomed's.

I climbed down and sat beside Dave on the bench. A few third-stringers who'd probably never get in the game were doing push-ups behind us.

Dave said, "We're not going to have much of a cheering section if everyone's reading."

"Leah will take care of that," I told him. "Wait until Leah gets out there."

Then I said, "If you bought a copy, where is it?"

"In my locker."

"Let's see it," I said.

"You wouldn't spend a dime, but you'd look at somebody else's copy, right?"

"I don't care that much," I said, but Dave was getting it out of his locker, still grumbling over the fact he'd spent the money, and now I was going to read it.

"Never mind, then," I said.

"Oh, look at it," he said. "You're dying to see it."

"Absolutely not," I said, but he'd spread it across our laps and I looked down at the front page.

There was a picture of a nun. Honest to God, a nun!

Above her photograph were the words: *REMOTE salutes.* . . . Underneath the picture, the words: HÉLOÏSE, niece of the medieval Canon Fulbert of Notre Dame Cathedral. Then these sentences:

> *Héloïse was one of the three outstanding female scholars of the Middle Ages. Beloved by Pierre Abélard, a monk, she married him in secret and gave birth to his son. Fulbert had Abélard emasculated by hired ruffians; Héloïse entered a nunnery. After the death of both lovers, their bodies were laid in the same tomb.*

That was the entire front page.

"What rubbish!" I said. "Where's your girl's ad?"

"I don't know which one it is," Dave answered. "The want ads are all on pages three and four."

"Two pages of want ads? Doomed must spend a lot of time dreaming them up."

"They're all authentic. There's a notice to that effect in a box above them."

"And you believe it?"

Dave only shrugged and turned to page three. "They start here."

Well, I knew instantly who'd written the first one.

I said, "Who'd answer one of these?"

"I'd answer my girl's, if I knew which one it was," Dave said.

I looked through the rest of the ads. I was amazed. If it was possible to trust Doomed's claim that the ads were all authentic, it was not just the girls participating.

There were male ads, too.

I read all the ads quickly, looking for one which might jokingly have been written by Leah.

I couldn't find any one in particular that seemed to be hers.

"These are pathetic," I said. "They're all written by losers who don't have normal relations with people."

"My girl isn't a loser," Dave said.

"But *she* did it for fun, Dave."

"I don't know."

"Sure she did. Leah and some girls wrote some for fun, too."

"She's been acting funny lately," he said. "She's been reading poetry, stuff she doesn't even have to read for English."

"Girls like poetry," I said. "I even like it."

"You know what she wanted me to do?"

"What?"

"She wanted me to get her a bunch of a-nen, an-nen—"

"Anemones?" I asked.

"Yes. She wanted me to buy her a bunch to carry to the game today. She said a lot of the girls are going to carry them."

"I doubt that five girls will carry anemones to the game today," I said.

"I doubt it, too," Dave said. "None of the florists have any left. I checked. They were sold out by noon. They said there was a run on them."

"A run on anemones?"

"I know. It surprises the florists, too. They said they were going to order some more."

"This is getting ridiculous!" I said.

Then Coach Luther made his grand pre-game appearance.

You were always able to smell the coach, on game days, before you saw him.

Today was no exception. The locker room smelled like a bottle of spilled whiskey.

"What are you retards sitting around in here for?" his voice boomed. "Get out on that field and limber up!"

Dave said to me, "He's his old self, I see."

"Bennett! McKee!" He shouted at us, heading for us with wild eyes, "What do you think this is, the library?"

Dave began folding up his copy of REMOTE when the coach snatched it from his hand.

"What are you reading?" he demanded.

"It's called REMOTE," I said.

He looked at it for a moment, and we waited for him to make his next nice, delicate gesture, like wadding it up and stuffing it down our throats. But a few beats passed, and another, and then he said, "Is this the Stein boy's newspaper?"

"Yes," I said, turning my head so I didn't gag on his breath.

As though he could read my mind he began

popping the mints he always carried into his mouth—rocking back and forth on his heels, turning the pages.

"I'm going to confiscate this," he said, and then he actually smiled again, and he folded the paper and put it under his arm.

"I didn't know there was a law against bringing a newspaper into the locker room," Dave said. It was brave of Dave to talk up like that, but Dave had always been known to be careful with a dollar, and a dime was a tenth of a dollar.

The coach just kept grinning as though that were the normal position for his mouth. "You'll get it back if we win, McKee," he said, "so get your ass out on that field and limber up!"

So the coach was not all *that* changed: he still climbed halfway into the bottle before a game, and he still had his mean mouth. But he was smiling, that was new. And he actually wore a new white trench coat.

Also, since when was the coach interested in a student newspaper? Very simple. Since the student was Stein, and since the coach had decided a certain Catherine Stein might be able to cope with his personal devil, booze.

I'll never know how we beat Moravia, but we did. The famous Leogrande didn't break anyone's bones, but our lead quarterback fell and broke his collarbone five minutes into the action, and near half time the guy who replaced him turned his ankle. We fumbled two of our new plays, and for some reason I couldn't have even tackled my own friendly collie dog that day, if he'd come tripping down the field.

The cheering was way, way off. If we'd depended on that muffled expression of school spirit for inspiration, we'd have lost hands down.

The thing is: Moravia wasn't on home ground, and their own cheering section was way, way off, too. The kids from Moravia had never seen anything like REMOTE, and they were passing it around and talking about it, and a lot of the guys actually credited REMOTE with Moravia's lack of enthusiasm.

They'd bussed in about fifty students for support, but it sounded more like fifteen when the cheerleaders got them rooting for poor old M.H.S.

I personally believe Moravia was just having a real streak of bad luck that afternoon . . . but I won't argue that REMOTE didn't play any part in the event. When you play on enemy territory, you really need reassurance, I know that. You don't need your classmates all preoccupied with

WANTED

A girl who plays guitar to telephone me once . . .

or

A male chauvinist to order me around for one date, and only one. ...

After the game we were all whooping it up in the locker room, when the coach appeared.

"You played lousy!" he barked at us. "You won because there's such a thing as an occasional miracle!"

He'd already burned a cigarette hole in his new trench coat, and managed to get grass stains on the back of it. But I'd seen him less sober on game day (particularly on the rare game days when we won), and I'd heard him say worse things to us when we'd played better than we had that day.

He walked over to Dave and returned RE-MOTE.

I expected him to say something like, "Here's your lousy newspaper, stupid," but all he said was, "This belongs to you."

"What did you think of it?" Dave asked him.

The coach shrugged.

Someone else said, "They say everyone on the Moravia side was reading it, and that's why Moravia didn't have any spirit."

I said, "I suppose we ought to send for Stein and congratulate him."

Then the coach said, "Stein didn't come to the game."

"He didn't even come to the game!" Dave said. "But he sent his salesmen to sell his newspapers! Oh, that's real school spirit."

"Stein's out of town with his father this weekend," the coach said. "He'd have been here, otherwise."

"I doubt that." I meant to say it under my breath, but it popped out in the open.

"And I doubt that you're a tackle," the coach said to me. "You looked more like a chicken with his head cut off this afternoon!"

Touché, touché.

I went into the showers and began looking forward to the evening. Leah and I were double-dating with Sophie and Carleton Penner.

I don't have the strength right now to describe Carleton Penner. That will come in the next chapter. I'll just warn you ahead of time that if you plan to go on to the next chapter, find some kind of medical encyclopedia and keep it close by. You'll need it.

Nine

That night as I was dressing for my date, I overheard my mother and my grandfather talking downstairs.

". . . and ever since that letter arrived," my mother said, "I've felt so sorry for him."

For a few crazy seconds I thought my mother meant me, and so did my grandfather, because he answered, "Alan takes things in his stride."

Then my mother said, "I don't mean Alan."

My grandfather gave one of his famous, long, exasperated sighs. He said, "Why on earth would you feel sorry for *him?*"

"Because I know him so well, I guess. Because he's always been so very weak."

"He wasn't very weak when it came to getting what he wanted, no matter who had to pay, and how."

"Yes, he was," my mother said. "He was acting out of weakness."

"You women always have to believe it's weakness and not just plain willful selfishness!" my grandfather said.

"I remember something from a Tennessee Williams play," my mother said. "I think it was *Cat On A Hot Tin Roof*. 'Oh, you weak, beautiful people who give up with such grace. What you need is someone to take hold of you—gently, with love, and hand your life back to you.'"

Silence.

My grandfather cleared his throat. "He didn't give up with grace. He gave up with no thought to anyone but himself. Sometimes I think you're still soft on him."

"He was the only man I ever loved," my mother said.

I pulled on my jeans and let that sink in. It came as a complete surprise. No. It came as a shock. I never thought of my mother loving him that much. Whenever I thought about my father at all, I thought about him walking out on us, and leaving my mother to face the town . . . and the prospect of bringing me up without a father.

"Love" isn't a word that conjures up a vision of one's own parents. If you think of love at all, in connection with their feelings about each other, you think of it as something that might have had something to do with them a long time ago. But

93

you don't think of it as the same kind of love *you're* experiencing; they're too old, and in their day it was kid stuff, being in love. It wasn't deep, like it is now.

At least that was the way I thought, even after I overheard that conversation. I told myself that my mother is just this terribly sentimental woman who uses words differently than my generation uses them. Oh, maybe she did love him; maybe he was the only man she ever loved, but I doubted that her feeling toward my father would qualify her for the front page of REMOTE.

Still, it rattled me a lot, hearing her say that about my father. I finished dressing, telling myself that the world would be much better off if they could boil down this "love" business to one meaning. It ought to be a simple enough thing to do.

I made up my own formula. I love Leah. Leah loves me. We love each other. Now, it's that easy, I told myself. If I leave Leah, that isn't love. If Leah leaves me, that isn't love. If we leave each other, that isn't love.

If you want to know, I was pretty sick and tired of the whole subject by the time I arrived at the Penningtons'.

Sophie opened the door for me. "Do you have any aspirin on you?" she asked.

"Why would I be carrying aspirin around?" I

said. "Doesn't your family have any in the medicine cabinet?"

"My family doesn't have pills of any kind in the medicine cabinet," Sophie said. "We might as well be Christian Scientists!"

"Well, I don't carry aspirin around," I said. "Who needs it?"

"Carleton," Sophie said. "He's downstairs in the rumpus room."

"Is he sick?"

"He's in pain," Sophie said. "Leah's still dressing. Go down and keep Carleton company while I run next door for aspirin."

"Where are your folks?" I said.

"Out."

"Maybe we should all stay in."

Sophie went out the door without acknowledging my remark.

I went downstairs to the rumpus room. The hi-fi was playing and there were three lighted candles stuck in the necks of old king-size Coke bottles.

At first I didn't see Carleton Penner. Then I saw this huddled ball of flesh and bones under a blanket on the couch.

Carleton Penner: medium height, thin, ears sticking out from his head like two large bureau-drawer pulls, brown eyes too close together, and a tendency toward buck teeth. Brown curly hair like a girl's frizzy, dime-store-kit home perm. My age.

"How do you feel?" I asked him.

"Turn down the music," he said.

I turned down the music, remembering the day Carleton Penner fainted in the cafeteria line, knocking down three girls, with their trays, behind him. They had to carry him into the school nurse's office. The school "nurse" was really only a dietitian, and Carlton kept screaming that no one was to examine him but a bona fide medical authority. He thought he had something called "extrasystoles."

"What seems to be the trouble?" I asked.

"I think it's only lumbago," he said, "but it could work itself into sciatica."

I sat down on the leather hassock. "Sophie's getting you some aspirin."

"I noticed a stiffness upon waking this morning," he said.

"I don't know anything about symptoms," I said.

"I do, though," he said. "It could just be a strain on the ligament between two vertebrae . . . but it could also be a partial slipping of the disc."

I noticed that he was clutching a hot-water bottle.

"How long have you had this pain?" I said.

"Since I got here," he said. "Just after I arrived."

Then I noticed the fresh bunch of anemones in a water glass on the table.

I said, "Where did these come from?"

"I brought them," he said. "I kept them overnight in our refrigerator. Sophie said not to come without them. I bought them yesterday."

Leah appeared then and grabbed me around the waist. Mmmmmmmmmm, you smell good," she said.

"I had two showers today."

"How do you feel, Carleton?" she asked.

"Well, I still have a dull, nagging backache. Not severe, but recurrent," he said.

"We were going to stay in, instead of going to the movies," Leah told me, "but it looks like we'd better go to the movies, after all."

"Why?" I said. "We never get a night here without your parents!"

"I know it," she said, "but Carleton's feeling bad. He may have to go home."

"So what?" I said.

"I probably will have to go home," Carleton said.

"It wouldn't be the same with Sophie here," Leah said. "Sophie doesn't want to be the third wheel."

Sophie arrived with the aspirin. "What's this about a third wheel?"

"I probably better go home," Carleton said.

"We'll all stay here," Sophie said. "I brought you aspirin."

"I'm not going to get better," he said. "I can tell that."

"Let's go to the movies, Leah," I said.

"Call me a taxi," Carleton said.

"Give yourself a *chance* to feel better," Sophie said. "Lumbago is often psychological in origin."

"Let's go to the movies, Leah," I repeated.

"I better go home right now," said Carleton, sitting up.

Sophie said, "Hey, wait a minute. Are you afraid to be alone with me? Are you trying to avoid normal social intercourse?"

"I can't have intercourse with a backache!" Carleton said.

"SOCIAL intercourse! SOCIAL intercourse! SOCIAL intercourse!" Sophie screamed at him. "I didn't say SEXUAL intercourse. I don't even want SEXUAL intercourse! I particularly don't want it with YOU!"

Carleton got up. He moved across the room toward his coat with difficulty. "I can't take this kind of pressure," he said. "This kind of pressure is an aggravant!"

"I'll call you a taxi!" Sophie stamped back upstairs.

Carleton struggled into his coat. "When I got here I was prepared to double-date for the movies," he said. "Everything's been blown way out of proportion."

Sophie was upstairs leaning over the banister, listening.

She called down, "I knew your lumbago was psychological in origin! You're afraid of girls!"

"I'm as normal as she is," Carleton muttered.

"That's not very normal," I told him.

That was how Leah and I ended up dropping off Carleton Penner in a taxi. Sophie stayed behind, locked in her bedroom.

We got off in front of Carleton's house, too, because we didn't want to pay extra for the taxi to take us four blocks into town.

"I hope you feel better, Carleton," Leah called to him as he went up the walk.

"I don't see how you two could be twins," he said. *"You're* nice."

"The anemones are really beautiful, Carleton," Leah said.

He gave a wave of his hand and said, "I'm glad someone enjoys them."

Then I noticed that Leah was carrying the damn anemones.

"What did you bring those along for?"

"For fun," she said.

"You're just going to carry them into the movies like that?"

"Sophie doesn't care. She said she didn't want to see them again."

99

"I care, though," I said.

We were walking down Garden Avenue having this testy little argument when something strange happened. I was listening to Leah, but I was looking straight ahead at a blue Triumph convertible which had just turned the corner and passed us. It was headed away from us, but not so fast that I didn't catch a glimpse of the coach and Catherine Stein.

Leah was saying, ". . . wish you had a sense of humor. A lot of the girls are carrying anemones places. It doesn't mean anything."

I was remembering what the coach had said that afternoon about Doomed being out of town with El Unbelievable.

"Does it?" Leah asked.

"Does what?"

"Does it mean anything?"

I sighed. "I don't know," I said, but I didn't mean that I didn't know if carrying anemones places meant anything.

What was strange was that I didn't say anything to Leah about what I'd just seen. I'd never said anything to her about seeing the coach at Lushing Brook that Tuesday morning, either.

"Why are you so quiet, Alan?" Leah asked me after we'd walked a block in silence. "Does it really bother you that I'm carrying these?"

"Nothing really bothers me, I guess," I said.

"Are you still thinking about your father's letter?" she said, taking my arm.

"I'll probably go see him, after all," I said.

"How come, Alan?"

"I don't know," I told her honestly, because what I'd just decided was news to me, too, "I suppose I'd better start trying to understand human weakness. There seems to be a lot of it around."

For some reason, after a minute or two, Leah just tossed the anemones away—and even though I hadn't been thinking about anemones at all, I was glad she'd done it.

Ten

I never told you which ad it was that Leah wrote for REMOTE. It was this one:

WANTED

Someone with ESP to sense who I am and what I feel about life. When you receive my vibrations, walk up to me and say "violet" and I'll be yours forever. Box V.

I thought it was a great ad. Leah told me about it that Saturday night when I made the decision to visit my father.

I wrote my father and told him I'd prefer to come Thanksgiving weekend instead of Christmas. For one thing it'd be over with quicker, and for another I couldn't imagine being away from home during the Christmas holidays. My mother always makes a fuss over Christmas, and Leah and I always have a lot of parties to attend together.

I also found out where Doomed and Dr. Stein had gone that weekend. El Unbelievable, in addition to drying out drunks, makes a tidy sum lecturing on contemporary problems. He and Doomed had gone to Chicago, where Dr. Stein delivered a lecture on "Changing Life-styles."

My grandfather clued me in on this information; my grandfather books guest lecturers for Rotary. One November evening I came home to find my grandfather staring hard at two photographs of El Unbelievable.

"Tell me something, Alan," he said. "Is there a difference between these two photographs of Dr. Stein?"

"Sure," I said. "He's holding a pipe in one and not in the other."

"I know that. I know that," my grandfather said, "but is there any other difference?"

"I don't think so."

"I don't think so, either, but Dr. Stein thinks there is. He wants us to use the one with the pipe."

"For what?" I said.

"I've booked him for next Tuesday's Rotary meeting. We're going to publicize it, since he's a local businessman. There'll be posters in all the store windows."

My grandfather told me he'd had lunch with Dr. Stein, and they'd discussed a lot of things, including the Chicago trip. Dr. Stein said he liked to take Doomed along, so Doomed could see new places and meet new people.

I still wanted to force my grandfather to make some kind of statement about my father, and my father's wish to see me. So far, he had kept his mouth shut on the subject.

So I said, "That's why it'll probably be good for me to visit New York. I ought to see new places and meet new people myself."

My grandfather's answer: "Yes, Dr. Stein is a very interesting fellow. It's too bad you don't take to his boy."

"His boy is just about ruining the senior year for all of us at school," I said.

"With that newspaper of his?" My grandfather chuckled.

"Yes, with that newspaper of his!" I said. "Nobody's behaving normally anymore. Everyone's posing. Everyone's playing hard to get, or pretending they have these tragic feelings—it's boring!"

"The point is, it's successful," spoke America's Number One Merchant and Rotarian, "and that means it fills a need."

What need was that, I wondered? What need could actually turn skinny little Gwendolyn Graney into the new school siren, and inspire two full pages of lost-sheep bleats? There was still a run on anemones at the local florists, too. Because anemones were expensive, the girls had taken to buying just one, and pinning it to their sweaters.

The day after my talk with my grandfather, I met Doomed by the water fountain in school. He'd just finished combing his twelve coal-black hairs, and he'd set about cleaning those weird rimless glasses of his. I said, "Keep yourself pretty, Stein—you never know when you'll run into Miss Right."

My grandfather was always talking about "Miss Right" and "Mr. Right." He always ignored the fact I planned to marry Leah, and told me I should do this or that because one day I'd finally meet "Miss Right," and then I'd be glad I knew how to play the piano or speak another language like a native. He'd come into a room where I'd be flopped on the floor watching television and pigging it with a bag of potato chips, and he'd say, "To think that in the far future *you'll* be someone's Mr. Right!"

Doomed looked at me with one of his cynical smiles and said, "There *is* no Miss Right, Bennett. The world will keep her from us."

"Funny," I said, "I've met her already and it hasn't bothered the world one bit."

I felt it was a good exit line, and I sauntered away from him without waiting to hear his answer.

A few minutes before I was due to report to

chemistry class, I ran into Sophie in the hall. She was very definitely not herself. She was wearing her regular glasses, not the dark ones. She was all smiles and she actually touched me affectionately, which is to say she gave my arm a little punch.

"Guess who I met in living color today!" she said.

"I give up."

"El Unbelievable! I had to go to the eye doctor during lunch hour, and El Unbelievable was there. I lost my dark glasses, and I was going to get some new ones, but now I don't think I'm going to get new ones, because El Unbelievable gave me the most marvelous—"

"Slow down," I said. "You've been around Norman Putnam too long."

"Norman Putnam!" she said disgustedly. "I'm light years away from that blabbermouth."

"What marvelous idea did El Unbelievable give you?"

"Contact lenses!" she said. "Not the old kind I could never wear, but the new soft lenses. He wears them."

"Why?" I said. "He's not a sports star." The only reason I could think of for a man to wear contact lenses was if he played sports. I'd heard a lot of Olympic stars wear them.

"To look better, dummy!" Sophie said. "He's not called El Unbelievable for nothing!"

"He's called that because you dreamed the name up for him," I said.

"I wouldn't have dreamed it up if he'd worn glasses, though."

"Contact lenses cost an arm and a leg," I said.

"You sound just like my father's going to sound when I go home tonight and tell him I want these new soft lenses," she said.

"Where's Leah?" I said.

"Do you realize you're limited to one topic of conversation, and only one?" Sophie said. "Do you know what that's called?"

"Love," I said.

"Fixation," Sophie corrected me. "An abnormal attachment to one object."

During Chemistry the thought came to me that it was odd that El Unbelievable insisted on contact lenses for himself, at the same time allowing Doomed to wear those ridiculous eyeglasses. I suppose there's a point when a parent just gives up and faces the fact he's got a real lemon on his hands. I also mulled over what could be going on between the coach and Catherine Stein, and how that all fit in with what I was learning about El Unbelievable.

After last bell, before it was time for me to report for football practice, I spotted Leah by her locker.

I went up to her and said, "Violet."

"It is not raining rain to me," she said. "It's raining violets."

"Hey! We could make a great song of that. We could call it 'April Showers.' We could find some great singer named Al Jolson to put it over." Then I did a little imitation of everyone else's imitation of this old-time star Al Jolson, down on one knee, singing "Oh, April showers . . ."

When I was finished, Leah said, "You know something, Alan? That song was stolen from a poet named Robert Loveman. Honestly. Practically word for word."

"Oh well," I said, "it was a long time ago."

"Everyone knows the song but not the poem," she said.

"That's probably why the songwriter stole the poem. No one knew it."

"It's interesting," Leah said.

"I love you. Isn't that interesting?"

She didn't even seem to hear me. She said, "Funny how derivative people are."

"Huh?" I just stared at her. I didn't even know what the word meant.

"Never mind," she said. "Oh, never mind, Alan."

"What's the matter with you?" I said.

Then she smiled at me and seemed to shake off some peculiar mood she was in. "I'm fine. Really. Are we studying together tonight?"

"Sure," I said. "At my house, right?"

She handed me three books. "Would you take these home? Then I won't have to lug them over when I come."

I stuck the books into my book bag.

On my way to the gym, I tried to figure out what all that business meant about "April Showers." I tried to remember that word she'd used that I didn't know the meaning of. I was frowning as I walked into the locker room.

"I hope that frown means you're thinking hard about your future!" the coach's voice boomed out at me. Then he added, "Because you don't have one in football!"

I looked at him. There was that smile again. I wasn't surprised by what he'd said, but there was that smile. He was waiting for some kind of reaction from me, and I realized the coach was actually teasing, instead of chewing me out. I didn't know how to respond because I wasn't used to that kind of behavior from him. It was like an attack dog suddenly nudging his teeth at your wrist instead of digging in for your veins.

I shrugged and couldn't think up an answer. He finally walked away.

The dumb thing was, the son-of-a-gun actually made me feel guilty because I'd let him down or something, while he was practicing being a nice guy. I think I even felt sorry for him.

Then he was his old mean-mouth self on the

field, and we all worked ourselves to death until it was dark out.

When I got home that night, my grandfather was sitting in his armchair studying one of the photographs of El Unbelievable.

"I know you like the man," I said, "but aren't you carrying it to an extreme?"

"What do you think of this photograph of him?" my grandfather asked.

"I told you last night what I thought of it."

"Look at it carefully."

"Okay . . . it's the pipe one. What can I tell you?"

"It's a *new* pipe one," he said. "He sent it around to the store this morning. He wants this one on the poster, not one of the others. I just can't see that much difference. I just can't see what all this fuss is about—which photograph should go on the poster."

"Neither can I," I said.

My grandfather sighed and shook his head. "*Vanitas vanitatum,*" he said. "*Vanitas vanitatum.*"

Eleven

When Leah came over to study with me that night, I unpinned the anemone from her sweater and said, "You can't seem to arrive at an attitude where Doomed is concerned, can you?"

"Just because I was wearing the anemone?" she said. "That doesn't have anything to do with Doomed. It's sort of a fad."

"It's his fad," I said.

"Oh, who cares who started it?" she answered. "It's just a fun thing. Where's your sense of fun, Alan?"

"Let's get our studying over and talk about it later," I said.

She said there was something she wanted to talk with me about first. It had to do with the weekend coming up. She wanted to go with some other girls on a shopping trip to nearby Syracuse, stay there for dinner and a movie, and come back late.

"Why *this* Saturday?" I said. "It's the one Saturday we don't have a game scheduled, the one Saturday we could do something together during the day."

"I realize that," she said. "I'm sorry about it. But that's the reason everyone else is going to Syracuse—because there's no game."

"Why do you have to stay for dinner and a movie?" I said. "We won't even have the evening together!"

"Just this once, Alan," she said.

"Let's study," I said.

"You're mad, though," she said.

I was furious. "I'm not mad," I said. "I've got more important things to get all worked up about." I slammed down the Latin reader we were going to go over together and muttered, "*Vanitas vanitatum*—to think I'm angry at such a little thing!"

She gave me a kiss on the cheek. "I'm glad you're not mad," she said.

"My umbilical cord was cut a long time ago," I told her.

"I'll look up the assignment," she said.

"I'd just as soon have a night out to look around myself," I said.

"Turn to page fifty-eight, Alan."

I said, "I might find myself having a ball! It's

been a long time since I've been out looking around."

"Page fifty-eight," she repeated.

In the midst of Cicero, my mother came into the room.

"Telephone for you, Alan," she said.

I hadn't even heard the phone ring, I was so angry.

As I walked toward the living room, my mother followed me. She said, "Alan, it's your father."

I heard her perfectly well. I said, "Who?" I'd stopped in my tracks. I suddenly understood what it meant to break out in a cold sweat.

"Your father's calling from New York," she said.

I shrugged. "What's the big deal?" I said.

"I just wanted you to know, so you'd be prepared."

"Nobody around here thinks I've got any cool," I said.

I walked rubber-legged to the telephone. My hand was shaking as I picked up the phone. My mother discreetly disappeared. It took me a moment to be able to speak at all.

"Yes?"

"Alan?"

"Yes."

"This is your father."

"Yes."

"How are you, Alan?"

"Okay."

"Alan, I've been thinking. I won't be here Thanksgiving weekend."

"Okay."

"But why don't you come this weekend?"

"This coming weekend?"

"Yes. I'll meet your plane Friday night."

"This Friday night?"

"Yes. We could spend Friday night, all day Saturday, and half of Sunday together. You could go back Sunday night."

"Well . . ."

"It's all right with your mother. I checked."

"Yes."

"Is it okay with you, Alan?"

"Okay."

"I can't hear you, Alan."

"OKAY!"

"Fine, son. Great! Let me know what plane you'll arrive on."

"Yes," I said. "Good-bye."

I hung up, and just stood there shaking.

My mother came up behind me and put her arm around my waist. "Is it all right?"

"Why not?" I said.

"Are you going down Friday night?"

"Yes."

"Would you and Leah like milkshakes? I can fix some in the blender—"

"If you want to," I said.

Then I walked back on the same rubber legs to the sun porch, where Leah and I were studying.

"You look like you've seen a ghost," she said.

"We won't be seeing each other Friday night, either," I said.

"What's up?"

"Nothing," I said. "I'll probably run down to New York City to see my alleged old man."

"Really?" Leah said.

"Don't make a big deal out of it!" I said. "It's just a fun thing. Where's your sense of fun?"

Of course my big scene came later. I've never been one to deny myself a big scene. Half the time I don't know how much of it is me, and how much of it is an act. I walked Leah back to her house after we'd studied, and she managed to coax me out of my silence, and get me to talk a little about this grand reunion with Mr. K. Kinney. I got all choked up with self-pity, and we sat on the Penningtons' front steps for so long Mrs. Pennington blinked the porch light three times.

"He called me 'son,'" I complained. "He actually called me 'son.'"

"Maybe I won't go to Syracuse with the girls," Leah said. "I don't feel right, off having a good time while you're going through a crisis."

"You felt just fine about doing it when I wasn't going through a crisis," I said. "Don't do me any favors now."

"I just feel so helpless, Alan, and I want to help."

We faded into a clinch on that line, and right on signal, Sophie threw open the front door.

"Do either of you know the meaning of the word paralogia?" she demanded, while we were still fastened together. "It's an inability to reason clearly, because of a pathological condition of the cortex of the cerebrum! Mother has blinked that light three times at you, Leah!"

"I'm coming," Leah said.

"You look like you're waiting for an engraved invitation!" Sophie said.

"She's coming, Sophie," I said.

"This is a ten-thirty night for her," Sophie told me, "and it's almost eleven now!"

"I thought you weren't your sister's keeper," I said.

"I'm acting on my mother's orders!" Sophie shouted.

Sophie rattled us so, that I even forgot to return Leah's books to her. I carried them back to my house in my book bag. Two days later they were on the plane to New York City with me—that's how organized I was for the Big Rendezvous.

When I deplaned at Kennedy Airport and walked toward the exit gate, I saw him right away. My mother had no recent pictures of him, but I knew him from the old ones. I might have spotted him even if I hadn't seen some old photographs. He was standing there lighting one cigarette from another, watching the ramp like someone on Death Row waiting for the executioner, beads of sweat dotting his forehead.

He was very New York-looking, like the celebrities that come walking out on television talk shows. I don't know exactly how to explain it, except to say he looked rich and successful, and he had a tan in November. When he waved at me (I was the only kid on the flight, so he didn't have any trouble spotting me) I saw a glimmer of gold at his cuff, and another glimmer of gold at his belt buckle. He had on an expensive-looking sports coat, dark blue flannel slacks, and these suede shoes with gold buckles. He was taller than I am, and I could see his light blue eyes all the way across the room. His necktie matched his eyes; he did the same thing I did—chose colors to pick up the color of his eyes.

When he embraced me, I just stood there stiffly, and he soon let go of me.

"How are you, Alan?"

"Okay."

"I thought we'd have dinner together, then go back to the apartment and get you settled."

"All right."

"Anything special you'd like to eat?"

"Steak's all right," I managed.

"You like a good steak, hah?" he said, as though

it was some sort of fabulous discovery about my innermost personality. Then he punched my arm like we were old comrades and said, "So do I!"

He bought me the first drink I'd ever had out in public. I'd tasted my grandfather's Manhattans, and my mother's Seven-and-Sevens, but I'd never had my own cocktail. (I'd also drunk whiskey from flasks at dances and parties, without being overly impressed with the taste.)

He ordered me a rum collins in a restaurant called Old Homestead Steak House, which was really crowded and noisy. I was glad it was, because we hadn't done much talking on the way in from the airport. In fact, it had been a very painful ride, with my father finally getting into this long, desperate conversation about traffic problems with the cab driver.

After the waiter brought our drinks to the table, my father told me we were eating in the oldest steak house in New York. He said he'd decided I could have a drink for the occasion, even though I was underage.

He said, "You certainly look eighteen. You're very much the young man."

I felt like asking him what he thought I'd be, but I just said thanks and began gulping my drink. It tasted like spiked lemonade.

He said, "Hey, not so fast. There's alcohol in that."

I said, "I've had Manhattans and Seven-and-sevens before."

He said, "You don't drink a lot, though, do you?"

"I'm not an alcoholic," I said.

He laughed very hard at that. Then he seemed to think it over, and he said, "The subject of alcoholism isn't funny."

I said, "We have a place in Cayuta where drunks dry out."

"What do you mean?" he said.

"We call it Lushing Brook," I said, and then I loosened up a little and told him about Rushing Brook.

At one point, as we were eating our steaks, he said, "Your mother's done a good job."

I said, "We've managed fine."

He must have signaled the waiter for another round, because the waiter put another drink in front of me, and another double martini in front of him.

He took a gulp of it and said, "Have you given much thought to college, Alan?"

"I'm going to Syracuse University," I said.

"Is that where you want to go?"

"Yes," I said.

"Because if you want to go somewhere else, if it's a matter of money I—"

I interrupted him. "Syracuse has a good journalism school. I'm going to be a writer."

"Oh?" he said. "A writer! Well! *I* do some writing. Advertising writing, but—"

I interrupted him again. "I wouldn't write advertising," I said. "I'm not interested in commercial writing."

"You're going to be another Thomas Wolfe, hah?" he said.

"Who?" I said.

"You're going to be another J. D. Salinger, hah?" he said.

"I know who Thomas Wolfe is," I let him know.

"So you're going to write books," he said.

I nodded and drank down my rum collins.

He said, "You're supposed to sip those drinks, not chug-a-lug them like beer."

Then he chug-a-lugged his double martini, and signaled the waiter for another. "Just the martini this time."

I don't know what we talked about through the rest of the meal. I wasn't paying much attention. I was wondering why I'd ever come to New York, and how I'd ever get through the weekend. The thing was, I didn't like or dislike him, but I didn't know him, and I didn't see what we had to do with each other. I wasn't used to talking with complete strangers, either. I'd never been in the company of a complete stranger that long before, and I'd run out of things to say. I wasn't used to sitting around in a restaurant drinking rum collinses and eating a steak that three hungry dogs would have trouble finishing. I kept thinking: what am I doing here?

"Are you enjoying your meal?" he said.

"Yes."

"This is the oldest steak house in New York, Alan," he said.

"Right," I said.

"Do you eat out a lot in Cayuta?"

"We can't afford it," I said, going for his gut. Right after he left my mother, he sent her regular checks for about a year. Then he stopped. My grandfather was always trying to get my mother to take him to court, but she never did. She always said we'd manage. Somehow, we did.

"We're going to have a talk about money this weekend," he said.

"I don't want any," I said. "I managed . . . we manage."

We were finishing dinner when he was served his fourth double martini.

"I don't really need this," he said, tossing it down, calling for the check. Then he said, "Why didn't you eat all your steak?"

"I'm stuffed," I said. It was something I never said, something I knew better than to say, but I said it, anyway. My grandfather always said that saying it at the end of a big meal was just as bad as burping.

When we left the restaurant, my father pulled

me over to look at the sign outside.

"You see?" he said. "It's New York's oldest steak house—1868." Then he stuffed some matchbooks from the place into my coat pocket. "These are souvenirs," he said. I noticed that his speech was suddenly thick, and he was slurring.

My father lives in a penthouse apartment on Gramercy Park. When we got there, Pam answered the door. Behind her, the Hide-A-Bed was already pulled out in the living room. My father didn't even introduce us right away. He just said, "Why did you pull out the Hide-A-Bed, for Chrissake?"

"I thought—" Pam started to explain.

"You *didn't* think!" he said. "What did you think, that Alan was going to be put to bed immediately after dinner, like some—" he didn't finish the sentence. He threw my suitcase and my book bag down and said, "This is Alan."

"Hello, Alan." She held out her hand.

I shook her hand. "I don't care about the Hide-A-Bed," I said. "In fact, I'm tired."

"You *see?*" my father said to Pam. "He thinks he's supposed to go to bed!"

"I don't think that," I said, "but I wouldn't mind."

"You *see?*" my father said to Pam again.

Pam. She wasn't what I expected. You'd think the woman your own father ran off with would look like a woman a man would run off with, but Pam didn't look that way. She looked ordinary, like someone's mother—even more like someone's mother than my mother. She looked older than my mother. She wasn't beautiful or sexy. She was just redheaded and freckled, and she could have been Gwendolyn Graney twenty years from then. She was a beanpole with a sort of scared little smile. She was embarrassed because my father'd chewed her out, too.

I said, "We had a steak in New York's oldest steak restaurant."

"I can never finish those steaks, they're always so enormous," she said. "Did you finish yours?"

"No." I smiled at her.

"How was your flight?"

"It was smooth," I said. "I got a good view of New York. It's really pretty, all lit up like that."

My father was making himself a drink. Pam was watching him nervously, over her shoulder, trying to pretend she wasn't that concerned with what he was doing. He was slamming ice cubes into his glass and making a lot of noise.

"How would you like a Coke?" she said.

"I couldn't put another thing in my stomach," I said.

It was the truth. I suddenly felt like heaving.

My father said, "Alan's going to be a writer."

"Wonderful!" Pam said.

"How could it possibly affect *you?*" my father said. "You don't read enough in a year to fill a postage stamp!"

Pam blushed with shame. "I guess that's right," she said softly.

I said, "One thing I'll never write is advertisements. I'd rather sweep out toilets."

My father pretended he thought that was the funniest joke he'd ever heard. He came waltzing forward with his drink, a little unsteady on his pins suddenly. He said, "Alan's going to Syracuse University."

"I've heard that's a good school," Pam said.

"Oh, you heard that, did you?" he said. "And just where did you hear that? Just where did you go that anyone was talking about a higher education?"

I couldn't look at Pam. I didn't want to see her face.

She didn't answer him.

My father said, "Why don't you go in and watch the boob-tube movie, per usual, and leave my son and me to talk?"

Then I knew I had to heave. I barely had time to ask Pam where the bathroom was. I just made it in time.

After I was in there for a while, she called in, "Are you okay, Alan?"

"I'll be all right," I said. "It was those rum collinses."

I heard my father shouting, "For Chrissake, leave a puking man alone! Don't you know *anything?*"

When I finally came out of the bathroom, they were off in their bedroom. I heard him growl something, and then I heard her say he should know better than to order drinks for me at such a time.

"He has enough to handle this weekend, without liquor," she said.

"What the hell has he got to handle?" my father shouted back. "I suppose you mean me!"

"Hush!" she said. "Please!"

"Then keep your trap shut yourself!" he hollered.

By the time they were finished arguing, I was into my pajamas. My father appeared and said, "Pam says good night. We can shoot the bull for a while, okay?"

"I'm too pooped," I said.

"Oh, come on," he said. "Let's let our hair down."

"I'd rather not," I said.

"Are you afraid to?"

"No," I said.

"Then shoot!" he said, starting to fix himself another drink.

"I don't know what you want me to say," I said.

He looked over his shoulder at me and smiled. "Just say what you think of things so far. How do things strike you so far about this visit?"

"I like Pam," I said.

"Huh?" he said. "You mean you like Pam better than you thought you would, ah?"

"No," I said. "I mean that so far it strikes me that I like Pam."

"What's that supposed to mean?" he said.

I got into the Hide-A-Bed without answering him. There was a light on the table beside the bed, and I snapped it out. The overhead light was still on. My father was standing at the foot of the bed. I turned on my side and pulled my knees up to my aching belly.

"What's that supposed to mean, you like Pam?" my father said.

I didn't anwer him. I couldn't see him because I had my eyes shut tight.

After a while the overhead light went out. I must have passed out within seconds, because the next thing I knew the sun was in my eyes.

Twelve

"How would you like some breakfast, Alan?" Pam said. "You don't have to dress. Just throw on your bathrobe and come out to the kitchen."

"What time is it, anyway?"

"Eleven o'clock," she said. "You had a good sound sleep."

I got into my robe and followed her out to the kitchen. It was about the size of a large closet, with just enough room for a table and two chairs. There was a small window looking out on a park across the street.

"Bacon and eggs?" Pam said.

"Thanks . . . is my father up?" I hated calling him that, but I didn't know what else to call him.

"Oh, he's been gone for an hour or more," Pam said. "He goes to his doctor Saturday mornings."

"Is he sick?"

She smiled. "No. He's got a little hangover, but that hasn't got anything to do with the doctor. The doctor's a psychoanalyst."

"That doesn't surprise me," I said.

She was fixing breakfast for us at the stove. She had on slacks and a shirt, and no makeup, which made her look somehow slightly younger, but very pale.

She said, "He feels bad about last night, Alan. Really. He had a lot to drink in a short space of time, and he was nervous about meeting you too."

"I don't see why he had to give it to you that way, that's all."

"I understood," she said. "He doesn't mean the things he says."

"I don't see why he has to say them."

"You're probably not used to that sort of thing," she said.

"What sort of thing?"

"Husband-and-wife fights," she said.

"*You* weren't fighting."

"He was right, Alan. I shouldn't have pulled out the bed. I did it without thinking."

"I think it was thoughtful of you," I said.

"Thanks, Alan. You're a nice guy, aren't you?"

"I just don't know," I said. "I don't feel like a nice guy."

"Tell me about Cayuta," she said. "You know it's my hometown, too."

I'd almost forgotten that.

She said, "I've lost touch with it, but I still think of it as my hometown."

We talked for a long time while we had breakfast. It was easy for me to talk with her. I guess it's always been easier for me to talk with a woman than a man, even my grandfather. I listen to my grandfather more than I talk to him. Even if I found it easy to talk with a man, I didn't see how I could ever have a decent conversation with my father, after the night before. He was just another bully, like the coach.

I told her a little about Cayuta, and a lot about Leah, but I stayed off the subject of my mother. She was the one who finally brought her up.

She said, "Your mother must be very proud of you."

"I don't know. I suppose she's pleased with the way I've turned out. It was hard for her, I guess."

"It was hard for your father, too, Alan, in another way."

"It was his choice," I said.

"Give him a chance, Alan," she said. "Don't judge him by last night."

"I just don't know what he wants, what he expects," I said. "I just don't think it's fair for him to expect me to behave like a son to him."

"He doesn't expect that. I think he'd settle for just being friends with you."

"If he were friendlier to you, I might be able to see it."

"We're very, very good friends," she said.

"It doesn't show," I told her.

"Try to understand something about husband and wife, Alan," she said. "They get to know each other so well, they get so used to each other's moods that they often dispense with the ordinary civilities. It probably isn't right, but it isn't as wrong as it seems to an outsider, either."

"Why is he going to a headshrinker?" I said.

"That's a question you should ask him, not me."

"I never will, though," I said.

It turned out that I didn't have to ask him. He offered the information himself. While we were finishing breakfast, he came charging in carrying a huge bouquet of flowers, a box of strawberries, and a copy of *The New York Times*. He presented Pam with the flowers, set the strawberries and newspaper on the table, then hugged Pam and reached across and mussed my hair. That didn't endear him to me, either. The only other person who ever mussed my hair was Lucius Luther.

Pam gave him a cup of coffee and he sat down with me while she did the dishes.

"I've been to my shrink," he told me. "Do you know what a shrink is, Alan?"

"Yes. Of course."

"Yes, of course you do," he said. "I shouldn't patronize you. Do you want some fresh strawberries?"

"I'm stuffed," I said.

"I've been going to a shrink to see what I can do about this low boiling point of mine," he said.

I didn't say anything.

"Oh, that's not the only reason I'm being shrunk," he said.

Pam said, "But that's a pretty good one for openers."

They both laughed.

"I'm sorry about last night," he said.

"Don't apologize to *me*," I said.

"I've already apologized to Pam."

I shrugged and drank my milk. I really wanted to shake off the bad mood the sight of him put me in. Okay, so he'd been mean to her—she didn't seem to hold it against him—why should I? But there was just something about him that made me unable to loosen up.

"I'm seeing a shrink because I've made a mess of things, I guess," he said.

My God, I didn't want to *hear* about it! Stuff it! I sat there like a prisoner. I couldn't even blow the scene if I felt like it, go somewhere by myself and wait until my mood changed . . . or his mood changed. I was trapped. Then, to make matters worse, Pam left us alone in the kitchen.

"I never used to be able to admit I was wrong about anything," he continued. "Now I'm hav-trouble admitting I'm right about anything."

I said, "I guess I'd better get dressed."

He looked at me with this disappointed expression in his eyes, but he didn't try to stop me. I got up.

"We're going to see a show tonight," he said. "Then we'll have dinner somewhere, wherever you want. What would you like to eat?"

"For *dinner?*" I said.

"That's right—it's too early to decide," he said. "We'll talk about it later. . . . Would you like to go to the Museum of Natural History this afternoon, Alan?"

"Okay," I said.

"If you'd rather do something else, just say so. We could go up to the Coliseum and see the winter sports show, if you'd rather do that?"

"Either one," I said.

"How would you like to shop for a new sports jacket?" he said. "I'll bet you could use a new jacket."

I could have, but I wasn't taking any bribes from him. I said, "I've got plenty of clothes."

I guess we were about halfway through the Museum of Natural History when I suddenly realized what an ass I was being. Since I wasn't planning on letting him into my life in the form of a father, why not follow Pam's suggestion and let him in as a sort of lukewarm friend? I had friends who were a lot worse than he was. I had friends who'd gotten bombed and behaved like much bigger rats too. The only reason I'd have for *not* forgiving him would be that I actually did think of him as a father. *No way.* I decided to snap out of it, and behave toward him the way I'd behave toward Dave McKee or any other guy I could take or leave alone. That made more sense.

I began to laugh at his jokes and crack a few myself, and we went from the museum to the Coliseum, and wound up at this fancy soda shop on Central Park South, eating banana splits.

"I haven't had one of these in years," he said.

"Neither have I," I told him. "In fact, I've never had one like this."

I never had, either. It cost two dollars and a half! I said, "Boy, is New York expensive!"

"Speaking of money," he said, "could you use a little extra every month, Alan?"

"Never mind," I said.

"I don't mean a lot, I mean—"

"I don't want any!" I said.

He looked at me for a moment. He said, "I'm trying to buy you, aren't I?"

"I don't know," I said. "Are you?"

"Yeah," he said, "and if I could, it'd be worth every cent."

"Cut it out," I said softly. He'd sort of gotten to me.

"If I can't buy you," he said, "can't I at least buy you a jacket, or something? What the hell,

Alan—you could use something, couldn't you?"

I'm not the Rock of Gibraltar.

We went to a place called Brooks Brothers, and I picked out a sports coat. It cost $125. I never had (then or since) such an expensive article of clothing, not even an entire suit that cost that much. I could picture Leah's eyes when she saw it. I think I have a lot of my mother in me, because that coat gave me the same kind of natural high she got when she'd come back from shopping in Syracuse, and she'd found a dress or a hat that she really liked. They say that everyone has a little of the queer in them, and maybe I'm faggy deep down about clothes, because I really felt good when we got back to the apartment. I'd never known that about myself, mainly because no one had ever taken me to a men's store and said, "Pick out anything you want."

The coat fit perfectly too, which meant I could wear it that night when I went out with my father and Pam.

My father and I were all smiles, and Pam could see the mood had swung, and she became very happy, too. We sat around the apartment talking for a while, and then they decided to take naps, and let me have some time to myself before we all dressed for the evening.

For a while I wandered around the living room, listening to the hi-fi, and looking at the view of New York from their windows. I kept wishing Leah was with me, and I even went so far as to fantasize a weekend when she'd come down to New York with me, and we'd stand there looking out of the penthouse windows together. I didn't get too deeply into the fantasy because I didn't feel it was fair to my mother. But I felt fine, just fine.

Whenever I feel great, I think something's going to happen as punishment. I'll go blind or deaf or wake up from the dream. That afternoon I decided my punishment would be that I'd flunk Latin and not graduate with my class. I made a dive for my book bag.

That was when I found it.

It was a very slim volume called *The Life of Charlotte Buff*. I realized it was one of the books I'd never returned to Leah. She'd given it to me that day she was planning to come over to my house to study. It wasn't a library book; it wasn't anything I could remember having been assigned to read. I opened the book and saw the name written inside: Duncan Stein. Then I saw the letter.

> *Dear Leah Pennington:*
> *Violet!*
> *I don't have ESP, but one of the advantages to being editor of REMOTE is that I know the names of the box holders. It is probably unethical for me to take this liberty,*

but I don't believe ethics matter when it comes to romance.

Furthermore, I sense who you are and what you feel about life, but I have no intention of asking you to be mine forever, and I hope you won't ask me to be yours forever.

Violet! I was going to borrow a verse about violets to include here—perhaps Robert Loveman's (1864-1923) "April Rain," except the writers of the popular song "April Showers" have already "borrowed" it and called it their own. Did you know that, Leah? Most creative people are either outright thieves or so derivative it's painful.

I would never aspire to be a novelist for that reason. Writers and would-be-writers are all dreary and derivative and end up drunkards. Rushing Brook is full of them, so I know.

Violet! Violet!

I will see you for one afternoon and evening, and only one afternoon and evening, this coming Saturday. Never after that. Call me to verify our first and last date. Meanwhile, enjoy this book about Charlotte Buff. REMOTE will salute her in the next issue.

Yours for a short time,
D.S.

P.S. No one need ever know. We can tryst in Syracuse. The limousine will take us there and back.

Thirteen

"Okay, what's eating you?" my father said.

We were in another packed New York restaurant after the show. Don't ask me what the show was about, or even the name of it—I can't remember. I sat through it like a bump on a log while everyone else laughed and clapped and had a fine old time. All I could think about was Leah, off somewhere in Syracuse with Doomed.

"Keep your voice down, Ken," Pam said.

My father was drinking, for a change. We were halfway through lobsters, but my father had stopped eating his, and was now smoking a cigarette and finishing his fourth or fifth martini.

"Nothing's eating me," I said. "I have a little headache." I sounded like Carleton Penner, and tried not to sound like him by forcing a chuckle and adding, "I think I'll live, though."

"I doubt that very much," my father said.

"Ken," Pam said, "Don't spoil things."

"I doubt that you know *how* to live," my father said. "It's my guess that you're like your mother, and you only know how to suffer."

Pam sucked in her breath and moaned, "Oh, *Ken*."

"Well, who's spoiling things? I'm doing the best I damn well know how! My son, The Silent Sufferer, is the one who's spoiling things!"

"I'm not like my mother," I said, because I damn well didn't like my mother suddenly brought into things. "*I* would have left *you*, and not the other way around." I tossed my fork into the mess of shells and lobster on my plate and stopped eating.

"Check!" my father called.

Pam said, "What suddenly happened between you two? I thought we were going to have a good time tonight—"

"He doesn't know how to have a good time," my father said.

"I know how to have a good time," I said.

"He only knows how to feel sorry for himself," my father said.

"Well I have a reason for feeling sorry for myself," I said, wanting to tell them suddenly about Leah and Doomed, wanting to try and straighten things out so they both understood.

But my father didn't want to hear any explanations. "You felt just dandy after I blew that wad on your jacket! Maybe you want some more graft to make you smile, hah? Five dollars for a smile, Alan?" He'd reached into his wallet and shoved money across the table at me. I shoved it back at him. "Stuff it!" I said.

People in the restaurant were looking at us.

"What suddenly happened?" Pam was saying in this bewildered voice.

The waiter brought the check.

"He's not comfortable in the role of human being, Pam," my father snarled. "He'd rather be strung up on the cross like a good martyr. His mother was the same way."

"Stop it right now!" Pam told my father. "Leave her out of it."

My father was on his feet, slapping bills down on top of the check. He charged up to the checkroom for his coat.

Pam just looked at me.

I was so angry I could hardly speak.

"What happened, Alan? Do you have a bad headache?"

"He's the headache," I said.

"But this afternoon things went so well—"

"How do you stand him?" I muttered.

"My God, Alan, can't you forgive and forget?"

On the way back to their apartment in the taxi,

my father treated us to a nice little drunken monologue. I knew I never should have let him buy me anything. He said no good deeds went unpunished, and he said the worm would always turn, and he called me a wallower in my own muck.

I had the distinct feeling Pam was on his side this time. Maybe the truth was that Pam had never been on anyone's side but his. Maybe that was what was wrong with him.

I might have been able to explain things to them, but not after the crack about my mother, or "the graft." I suddenly realized the guy really hated me: that was all. Misopedia, as Sophie would analyze it—a neurotic dislike of one's own child. I was glad I'd realized it before I'd started to explain that I'd been ditched by my girl. He'd have had a good time with that one! He'd have said I was playing the martyr, The Silent Sufferer —you name it.

"You like being a loser, don't you, Alan?" my father said.

"I don't know," I answered. "I haven't been one as long as you have."

He leaned across Pam and slapped my face.

Then the taxi stopped and we were "home."

We didn't speak going up in the elevator. My father's face was bright red and he was breathing very hard. I noticed Pam had her arm in his, and was holding onto him tightly.

My father made himself a drink and took it into the bedroom.

Pam started to pull out the Hide-A-Bed, but I told her that wasn't necessary, that I'd just sleep on the couch until morning, and then I'd go out to the airport and take the first plane.

For a moment, Pam looked like she was going to sit down and talk with me. For a moment, I thought I was going to ask her to, because I felt badly that she thought I was just this ungrateful clod.

She stood there lighting a cigarette with shaking hands. "I tried to give these up," she said.

I said, "It's hard to get through to him when he drinks."

"He thought you two were going to be friends. I thought so, too."

"We might have been, but we never will be now."

"Why don't you give him a chance?" she said. "He just wanted you to have a good time. He picked the show so carefully, hoping you'd enjoy it."

"It wasn't the show. It wasn't anything he did. Before I could tell him what it was, all this hatred came spilling out."

"Alan, he *loves* you!"

"He doesn't love *me*. He loves the idea that he has a son, and he hates it when I don't match up with his idea of a son!"

My father was suddenly in the room, answering me. "You don't match up with my idea of anything!" he said. "Oh, you were a big bullshit artist, all right, you were! You didn't want anything from me! You couldn't be bought, could you? Well, you could be bought. Took you to Brooks and bought you a damned coat, you little creep, and you were all smiles for about an hour! Here!" he threw some tens across the room. "Pick 'em up and act like a human being!"

Pam said, "Ken, stop it. Please."

"You're another crummy silent sufferer with your hand out!" he said to Pam. "You pick up the money, if you want it so bad! You can fight each other for the money!"

Neither Pam nor I answered him. I had the idea he was going to go for me, and it wouldn't be just a slap across the face. I stayed as still as I could, and Pam did too. We all three just stood there. He was weaving back and forth, holding an empty glass.

He turned to Pam. "You loved me because you were jilted and I rescued you!" he said. He looked at me. "You never loved me!" He dropped the empty glass on the carpet and looked down at it. "The only one who ever loved me for myself was his mother, and I didn't love her."

Then his face broke up like someone about to laugh very hard, only he was crying. "And I didn't love anyone," he sobbed. "It's too hard. I can't do hard things." He was bawling like a baby.

I sat down with this sick feeling in my gut, listening to his sobs.

Pam was saying, "Hush, darling! It's all right ... it is."

I didn't sleep that night; I didn't even try to. I packed and waited for morning. I sat around in their living room watching the sky grow blue.

All I knew was that I wanted to get out of there. I did, just as soon as it was light out, before anyone was up.

I took the bus out to the airport. There'd been some kind of convention in New York that weekend, and the morning planes to Syracuse were filled to capacity. They booked me on an afternoon flight around three o'clock.

I knew I couldn't eat, so I didn't order breakfast. I just wandered about for a long time. Around noon my conscience got the best of me and I called my father's number.

Pam answered.

I said, "I just want you to know I'm all right. I'm on my way back."

"I'm sorry the way things turned out," she said. "You left your coat behind. We'll send it to you."

"I didn't leave it behind accidentally," I told her. "Don't send it."

Then she said, "Don't you feel anything for him, Alan?"

"I feel sorry for him," I said. "It's too late to feel anything else for him. Like he says, it's too hard."

"Good-bye, Alan."

I said good-bye and hung up.

It dawned on me I hadn't thought about Leah once since the big explosion. I didn't feel at all like thinking about her.

Stuff it! Stuff everything!

I'd told my mother I'd let her know when I was coming back, so she could meet my plane in Syracuse. She'd said if I wanted to stay over Sunday night, she'd meet me early Monday morning.

I decided to let her think I was staying over, and just take the bus back to Cayuta on my own. I'd explain things when I got there.

The plane touched down in Syracuse around five that Sunday afternoon. I'd managed to sleep a little on the plane, so I felt less shaky when I arrived. I just wanted to splash some cold water across my face before I headed into town to catch the bus. I never managed to do this.

Just as I was approaching the men's room, I saw them. I'd noticed them from quite a distance, without knowing who they were. They were standing over behind a public phone booth, and she was crying very hard. He was sort of sheltering her from view. His right hand was bandaged. His left arm was around her shoulder, and her face was buried in his overcoat.

I stopped in my tracks when I saw the coach's face in profile. I didn't have to see her face to know who it was. I saw the long black hair.

I turned around and headed away in the opposite direction.

It was dark outside, but the overnight parking lot was brightly lighted. When I pulled away in a taxi, I saw the coach's little blue Triumph parked there.

They say there are some things you can't put in a novel because they don't ring true, even though they are. Mrs. Tompkins, our English teacher, says fiction isn't like life at all, because fiction can avoid all of life's bizarre coincidences, unravel all the mysteries of fate, and resolve everything in a neat package, as real life never can.

I'm always asking her if that means I can't write an autobiographical novel without discarding actual happenings which seem unreal.

She always answers: "All you can do is try and see if they come across in a believable way."

What happened to me next isn't going to be any more believable than it was when it took place. I don't know what to do about that except put it down just as matter of factly as The Fates served it up.

I had another two-hour wait for the bus to Cayuta. I bought a Ross Macdonald paperback mystery to read on the bus, and found out as I was sitting in the waiting room that I'd already read it. I ate two Milky Ways, for energy, while the bus was loading up, and then I leaned back and closed my eyes, wishing I had the guts to return the paperback to the newsstand in exchange for one I hadn't read.

I heard the bus door slam and the motor start, and then I opened my eyes when a voice asked, "Is this seat taken?"

Catherine Stein didn't recognize me until after she sat down beside me.

Fourteen

"Well," she said, "well . . . Albert Bennett."

"Alan," I said. "Alan Bennett."

"What a nice surprise. Did you spend the day in Syracuse?"

"I just got off the train from New York," I said.

"My hometown," she said slipping off her coat. "Did you have a good time?"

"Sort of," I said.

"Just sort of?"

"Well," I said, "I was visiting my father and I don't know him very well."

"Dunc was out of town this weekend, too."

"He was?"

"He still is," she said. "He went to Buffalo for his father. We're very proud of him. He filled in for his father this weekend. He had a speaking engagement last night, and this afternoon."

"He did?" I said. "In Buffalo?"

"Yes." She took out a cigarette. She scratched the match four times before it flamed. "I've been trying to give these nasty things up," she said.

"Everyone seems to be trying to do that," I said.

It was a half-hour bus ride from Syracuse to Cayuta. The bus was filled to capacity, mostly with soldiers returning to the base just outside Cayuta.

I said, "I didn't know Duncan gave lectures."

"This was his first time," she said. "He filled in for his father."

I wanted to ask her what had happened to El Unbelievable, but the same thing that made me say I took the train, instead of a plane, kept me from posing the question. I had an idea that somehow the coach was involved. I didn't want her to know I knew anything; I didn't want to make her uncomfortable.

For all I knew, Leah had gone to Buffalo with Doomed. I doubted it, because I knew how strict Mr. Pennington was. He might allow Leah to go to a movie with Doomed in Syracuse, with a chauffeur driving them, but I couldn't see him letting her go to Buffalo with Doomed on an overnight trip.

I decided to make sure of the facts. I said, "So Duncan stayed overnight in Buffalo?"

"What?" she said. "I'm sorry, Albert, I wasn't listening."

"I said I guess Duncan stayed overnight in Buffalo."

"Yes," she said.

She was smoking the cigarette with her eyes closed, her head leaning back against the top of the seat.

I took out the Ross Macdonald book and pretended to read it.

After a while she put out the cigarette. For a few minutes I turned the pages of the book, pretending I was engrossed in the story. She lit another cigarette.

Then she said, "I'm planning a surprise."

I said, "Oh?" I put my book down and glanced at her. She gave me a quick little smile and said, "My surprise would be spoiled if it got out that I was in Syracuse today."

"I see what you mean," I said. "Don't worry about me. I won't tell anyone." I added, "Not a soul. Believe me."

She said, "It's awfully hard to keep a secret. I know that."

I said, "It's not hard for me. I keep things to myself. I always have."

She pressed her palm against my wrist for a second. "Thank you," she said.

"No one's meeting me at the bus depot, either," I reassured her.

She said, "I'll get off at the Grant Street stop, anyway."

The Grant Street stop was just outside of Cayuta. Soldiers got off the bus there, to catch the base bus. It was a mile from center-town, in the heart of the huge shopping center.

"Did you have a good time in New York?" she asked again.

"I saw my father for the first time," I said.

"I love that city. I sometimes wish I'd never left it."

"It's a very big place," I said. "You can really get lost there. Not *lost* lost, but lost from all the things that bug you, unless the things that bug you are there."

"Even then," she said. "You can get lost there —even then."

"Yes, I guess even then," I said. "I didn't get along too well with my father, but after I cut out and went out to the airport, I didn't feel his presence the way I probably would have if I'd cut out in a small town and headed for the airport. I mean, in a small town he might have come after me or something, if he was the type who'd chase after me. Which he isn't. Which is just as well." That little talkathon would have done credit to Norman Putnam, I thought to myself when I'd finished.

" 'In the Big City a man will disappear with the suddenness and completeness of the flame of a candle that is blown out,' " she said. "O. Henry wrote that . . . I used to like to go to a restaurant called Petes, in New York. It's on Eighteenth Street. O. Henry used to sit at a table there and write his short stories."

"Did you ever meet him?" I asked.

She laughed. "I'm not quite that long in the tooth, Albert."

"I didn't mean anything like that," I said. "I just don't know much about O. Henry."

"He was an interesting man," she said. "If you're going to be a writer, you should read him."

It made me feel great that she remembered I planned to be a writer, even though she couldn't seem to get my name straight.

"I will read him," I said. "That's another promise to you I'll keep."

She glanced at me a little uncertainly.

I said, "I'll help keep your surprise a secret, and I'll read O. Henry."

She glanced away and put out another cigarette. I wondered if she was thinking of that Shakespeare line—"Methinks you do protest too much" —or something like that, meaning that if someone keeps insisting on something, it could be he doesn't mean it. Mrs. Tompkins sometimes threw that line at you when you were late with an assignment, and you kept talking about how you planned to hand it in very soon, how you just needed more time, how busy you'd been, et cetera.

I felt like blurting out I knew a lot already that I'd never told a soul. I ached to say, "Trust me," or "Catherine, I may be a lot younger and shorter in the tooth than you are, but I have a great affection for you. I'd never hurt you."

Instead, I went back to my mystery book, turning the pages without reading the words, making up little soliloquies in my head that I wished Catherine Stein would sense by vibration.

She had her eyes closed again, but I knew she wasn't asleep. She was wringing her hands together on her lap. She let out these tiny sighs. Ultimately she took out another cigarette.

She said softly, "I guess I'm out of matches."

I dug in my coat pocket as though I carried matches around—I just had a wish to answer her every need and I did it automatically without thinking. I found the matchbooks my father'd handed me Friday night as souvenirs.

I lit her cigarette for her and handed her the matchbook. She looked at the cover. "Did you have dinner here while you were in New York?"

"Yes," I said. "It's supposed to be New York's oldest steak house."

"Were you visiting friends in New York?"

I remembered something Sophie said once about what Freud, the top shrink, said. To tease somebody is to love somebody, or something along that line. I felt very loving toward this woman because she seemed to be in trouble, real trouble. Maybe I have a thing about rescuing women who are in trouble because my father was such a bastard toward my mother. I don't know. I leave the analyzing to Sophie.

But I decided to tease Catherine Stein a little. I said, "I wasn't visiting friends there. I was visiting my father. And my name's Alan, not Albert. I guess I'm making an ant-sized impression on you," and I gave a little chuckle, "because I've been telling you about it since we left Syracuse."

She didn't say anything.

I said, "Oh well, it's not the first time my pearls of wisdom have fallen on deaf ears."

Silence.

I looked over at her.

There were tears streaming down her cheeks.

I said, "Oh, look, I was only teasing. I was—"

She pressed her palm against my wrist again. "I'm sorry," she said. "I'm not good company." She took a handkerchief out of her purse.

"You're great company," I said. "Honest. I was just being smart."

"I was being selfish. Forgive me, Alan."

I sat beside her stiffly while she sobbed very quietly into her handkerchief. Then she sniffed and caught her breath, and straightened up in the seat. Her cigarette was burning to a smoky mess in the ashtray in front of us. I tried to put it out with my finger, burned myself, and flinched.

For some reason she started crying all over again, and continued crying softly while I dealt with the burning ashtray.

I picked up my mystery book and she finally rested her head back against the top of the seat. We were silent for a long, long time.

We were almost to the Grant Avenue stop when I couldn't stand the silence any longer. I turned to her and said, "Whatever's making you sad—I hope it'll turn out okay."

"Thank you, Alan. I'm sorry I put you in this position."

"You haven't put me in any position," I said as the bus slowed up for the stop. "When I got off that plane this afternoon, I felt rotten. Misery enjoys company, I guess because I forgot all about my own troubles. I mean, we all have troubles and it's good to be reminded of it. That's all." I shut up before I did another Norman Putnam monologue.

She looked at me for a long moment, very carefully.

"Grant Avenue!" the bus driver shouted.

She said, "You took a *plane* from New York."

"Did I say that?" I felt the blood rush to my neck and spread to my cheeks.

She moved into the aisle. There were soldiers behind her. She leaned across and squeezed my hand hard.

"Thanks, Alan."

Then she was gone before I could answer her.

When I got home, my mother and my grandfather were still at the bimonthly Sunday-night church supper. I made myself a peanut butter sandwich and wolfed it down with a few glasses of milk. Then I cut myself a slab of chocolate cake, and demolished that.

I went into the living room and dialed Leah's number.

"It's so good to hear your voice," she said. "How did things go?"

"Things were just fine," I said. "How did things go with you?"

"Things went just fine," she said.

"How was Syracuse?" I said.

"We decided not to go," she said.

I said, "Haven't you missed *The Life of Charlotte Buff?*"

"So you do have it, after all," she said.

"Oh yes, I have it. And the letter inside."

"I wasn't going to keep that date, Alan," she said. "I thought I might, just out of sheer curiosity, but after you got the call from your father, I knew I'd never go through with it. Honestly, Alan!"

"You didn't go through with it, because Doomed had to go to Buffalo," I said. "That's why you didn't go through with it!"

"I canceled the date with him even before that man beat up his father," she said. "Honestly, Alan, I did!"

"What man beat up his father?" I said.

155

"One of the patients," she said. "One of the drunks got out of hand and broke Dr. Stein's nose. His ribs are cracked and everything. It happened Friday night while Duncan was skating with Kim Lingerman. He took Kim to—"

I slammed down the receiver. *Duncan,* she'd called him. Not Doomed, anymore—*Duncan.*

I stood there putting the pieces of the puzzle together, suddenly recollecting the sight of the coach's bandaged right hand.

The phone rang, and I let it ring ten times before I broke down and answered it.

Leah said, "Please don't hang up on me, Alan! I love you! I told Duncan I wasn't going to keep the date—I told him Friday morning."

"Violet," I said snidely.

"My gosh wouldn't *you* be curious? I was just curious. I wouldn't have gone through with it."

"I don't have any reason to trust you anymore," I said. I was suddenly proud of myself for never telling Leah anything about the coach and Catherine Stein . . . protective, very protective.

"Alan!" Leah said, "Alan, you couldn't believe I *care* anything about Dunc!"

From Doomed to Duncan to Dunc was a long distance in a very short space of time.

"Alan?" Leah said. "Are you there?"

"I'm here." I wanted to think of some way to mention the coach, to see if there was any news concerning him.

"Come over, Alan, please?" she said.

"I have football practice tomorrow," I said. "I need to rest up for the coach's bullying."

"Since when?" she said. "Since when has Coach Luther stopped you from doing anything you really wanted to do?"

So there *wasn't* any news concerning him.

I said, "I have a lot to think about, Leah. I'll see you tomorrow."

"Aren't you even going to tell me you love me, Alan?"

"I don't know what the hell that word means anymore," I said.

Fifteen

My mother and grandfather stayed late at the church supper, because they didn't know I was back from New York. I went right to bed, but not to sleep. My thoughts were running in every direction, from Leah, to my father, to Catherine Stein. I'd meant what I said when I'd told Leah on the telephone that I didn't know what the hell the word "love" meant. Maybe I still don't, but that Sunday night it seemed to me that there was absolutely no safety in that word. I associated it with warning signs like "Thin Ice" and "Narrow Passage" and "Dangerous Crossing." The only thing my father had said to me that made any sense was that love was just too hard.

When my mother and grandfather came home, my mother opened the door of my bedroom and said, "Are you asleep, Alan?"

"Just about." I imitated a thick, drowsy tone.

"Do you want to talk?"

"Can't now," I said. " 'Morrow."

But the next morning, I didn't feel like going into it. My mother and my grandfather and I had breakfast together.

"All I really want to say now about my trip to New York is that I'm glad it's over," I told them.

"We'll await the next bulletin suspensefully," my grandfather answered.

"Oh, *Dad,*" my mother said, "don't be so flippant."

"Are we supposed to hang suspended before Alan decides to communicate with us?" he said. "Boy doesn't even let us know when he's arriving. I call that being a little too independent."

"I just don't want to talk about it now," I said.

"Then don't!" my grandfather said. "And we can do without the teasers, like you're glad it's over. Say something or don't say anything."

"Your grandfather's worried about the Rotary luncheon tomorrow," my mother said. "Duncan Stein is going to fill in for his father, and your grandfather is worried that he won't be able to carry the program all by himself."

"He's going to talk on 'Communication Between Teenagers and Parents,' " my grandfather said. "He'll probably get up and say, 'All I really want to say now about communication between teenagers and parents is that I'm glad it's over.' "

I laughed in spite of myself. At least my grandfather is consistent.

Before I left for school, my mother took me aside in the hallway. "I'm glad you're back. I missed you."

"I'm okay, though," I said.

"You don't have to talk about it at all, unless you want to."

"I'll probably get around to it," I said.

The first person I saw as I went up the walk in front of Cayuta High was Sophie. It had snowed while I was gone. She was sitting by herself on a bench, bundled up inside a parka, studying chemistry.

"Why are you studying that out here in the cold?" I said.

"I suffer from ochlophobia," she answered.

"What's that?"

"A fear of crowds. Was your weekend traumatic?"

"Was yours?"

"Every day of my life is traumatic," she said, "particularly now that I'm launched on the big push for all A's. If I get all A's by June, I can have contact lenses. Now I suppose you want to know where Leah is."

"Not particularly," I said.

"Then don't bother me," she said. "I have the big push to worry about, as well as El Unbelievable's nose. Did you hear he broke his nose?"

"I heard someone broke it for him."

"I sent him a get-well card," Sophie said. "I signed it 'From the girl in Dr. Brewster's waiting room,' because our only contact was that day I met him there. I just hope he doesn't think it's from the receptionist."

"I doubt that it'll make any difference in his life either way."

"Do you realize that you've come back from New York cynical, sarcastic, and insensitive? Good·luck with your new personality, Alan Bennett."

While I was opening my locker, Kim Lingerman passed me wearing a wilted anemone pinned to her sweater, and a tragic expression on her long, horsey face. I vaguely remembered Leah telling me something about a skating date Doomed had taken Kim on. Then, on my way to Latin class, I ran into Carleton Penner. He was headed in to see the nurse-dietician about palpitations.

"I hope it's nothing trivial," I said.

"Thanks, Alan," he said, "I've probably set myself up for a coronary. I eat a lot of eggs."

Then I saw Leah. She was standing way down at the other end of the corridor, near the window. She was looking out, so she couldn't see me. Doomed was standing beside her. He was talking with her, and at the same time cleaning his glasses.

I ducked out of sight, and began suffering from palpitations myself. I just hated seeing Leah with that character. I didn't really suspect them of anything, but I didn't want Leah with him. She could be curious about, or friends with, anyone but Doomed. I just didn't like Doomed.

At noon, on the bulletin board outside the cafeteria, this notice was posted:

IN THE ABSENCE OF COACH LUTHER
FOOTBALL PRACTICE IS SUSPENDED
UNTIL FURTHER NOTICE

Behind me a voice said, "They say he's being interviewed for a new job, out of town."

I said, "Who are *they?*"

Leah smiled at me as I turned around and faced her. "It's just a rumor, I guess," she said.

"What are the other rumors?" I asked her. "What are the rumors about you?"

"There's one going around to the effect I love you."

"Is that an old one or an up-to-date one?"

"It's up to date," she said.

We ate lunch together, as we almost always did, but it was different. We were so polite with each other that it was like a first date. I kept looking at her and saying to myself: nothing's changed, *nothing* has. And she must have told me about ten times that she loved me, but it was like someone saying, "It's beginning to snow out," or "I'm glad it's a nice day." It sounded incidental and unimportant, like something you say to fill in pauses. There were plenty of pauses. We didn't even make a date to study together that night.

When I walked into English class, I could hear a buzzing all through the room. Everyone seemed to be in little knots whispering together. I sat down and opened my book and avoided looking at Doomed. I knew the moment he entered the classroom, because about half a dozen girls purred hellos at him. They were the same ones wearing those weeds pinned to their sweaters.

When Mrs. Tompkins came into the room, the buzzing died down a little, but it didn't stop. That was unusual.

Then Mrs. Tompkins said, "All right, quiet! I understand that you're upset, those of you who've heard the news. In case any of you haven't heard about it, I may as well tell you. Earlier this morning, Norman Putnam's father was killed in an automobile accident. He was bringing Norman to school. There was a rumor circulating that Norman was killed, too, but that was a false rumor. Norman is in Mercy Hospital. He's all right."

Mrs. Tompkins continued with the lesson, which was a study of Robert Browning's "Fra Lippo Lippi." It was hard for everybody to concentrate. Mrs. Tompkins realized this and she stopped the lesson a few minutes before the bell rang.

She said, "We haven't written a composition in some time. In the light of what just happened, I think it might be appropriate to assign a short composition on 'A Father I Know.' You don't have to write about your own father, though that would be ideal. Write something about a father's role, or your relationship with your father, or someone else's relationship with your father, or someone else's relationship with his or her father. Use your own judgment. The composition is due two weeks from today."

Beautiful, I thought, just *beautiful!*

There was a note from Leah Scotch-taped to my locker, which I found at the end of classes that afternoon.

Dear Alan,

I don't know what happened to you in New York, but you're changed.

Don't try to blame the change on that silly letter you found (since when do we read each other's mail?) or on the fact I was playing with the idea of satisfying my curiosity about Duncan. I love you, but that doesn't mean I'm not curious about other people.

Love shouldn't be a prison, anyway. If I love you, am I trapped forever?

> *Please answer!!!!!!!!!!!!!!*
> *Leah*

I wrote the following answer:

REMOTE SALUTES:
LEAH PENNINGTON
Her curiosity got her Doomed.

At the time, I thought it was a very snappy retort.

Sixteen

For the rest of that week, Leah and I avoided each other. Between classes, I'd go back to my locker, even if I didn't have to, and look for a note there. I never found one. I even began to believe she might have left one, and someone might have taken it. At night, I studied in the living room, right next to the telephone. When it didn't ring, I'd pick it up and listen for the dial tone, to be sure the phone wasn't out of order. At noon, I went home for lunch because I didn't want to just run into her casually. I wanted us to get back on some kind of footing before that happened. We had Latin and History together, but she was a P and I was a B, and we were seated alphabetically. I could see her, and hear her, but we kept our distance from each other. I began to put on an act for her benefit: always all smiles and whistling in the halls and hurrying around as though I had important things to do and think about.

My grandfather came home with a glowing report on Doomed's speech before the Rotary. He talked about it all week.

"He's a very mature young fellow," my grandfather said one night at dinner.

"He was born old," I said.

"Where's Leah been lately?" my mother asked.

"Lately Leah's been stubborn," I said. "We're having a contest of will."

"He has a very practical, sound approach to life," my grandfather continued. "He's a realist."

"He's about as realistic as I am impressed by him," I said.

"I was hoping you'd had a tiff with Leah," my mother said.

I said, "What? You were *hoping* I had a tiff with Leah?"

"I was hoping that was the reason you were coming home from lunch and staying to yourself so much," she said. "I was hoping something else wasn't bothering you."

"Duncan Stein wouldn't let some little gal get him down," my grandfather said.

"Right!" I agreed. "He has an adding machine for a heart. It's quantity with him, not quality."

"Quality is in the mind's eye," said Cayuta's leading merchant and organizer of half-price panty-hose sales. "It's a state of mind, and not necessarily a movable commodity. Quantity moves right along and quality dallies."

"Is poor Norman Putnam out of the hospital yet?" my mother said.

"He's due out Friday," I said.

My grandfather said, "Dr. Stein is up and about. His nose is bandaged up like a lunchroom hot dog to take out."

My mother laughed. "The way you put things, Dad."

"I should have been a writer," my grandfather said. "I just might become one yet. We could use a writer in the family." He looked across at me to see if he'd landed on target.

But I wasn't up to bantering with him. I was thinking about Catherine Stein. I'd been think-ing about her a lot. My head was divided into a triangle: Leah at one point, my father at another, and Catherine Stein. Leah, I believed, would come around eventually. My father, I believed, would stay completely out of my life. I was all for that.

Catherine Stein was the puzzle. I never found out any more details. I didn't know if Doomed knew about the coach; I didn't know if anyone did besides me, and Dr. Stein. I didn't know how the fight had happened or where or why. I could only guess that in some kind of confrontation the coach had broken El Unbelievable's nose, and I was pretty positive it had to do with whatever was going on between the coach and Catherine Stein.

The coach was still absent. I hadn't seen Catherine Stein since our bus ride together.

One of the things that occurred to me whenever I thought about Catherine Stein was what Mrs. Tompkins would call "an irony of sorts." It was that bus ride . . . and the fact that Doomed had first broken into print with his own little story in REMOTE about a bus ride with a girl, and its effect on him.

I was still weighing the effect of my bus ride with Catherine Stein. It had definitely had an effect, because during the week that followed I'd sometimes think about it before I went to sleep. I'd improve on it in my mind. I'd say and do the right thing, and we'd arrive at the Grand Street stop with this tremendous bond between us. I'd look out the bus window and see her looking back to wave at me. I'd light a cigarette (I smoked a lot in my fantasies) and watch it glow and remember her telling me: "Alan, I want to see you again. Don't forget me, will you?" Once I woke up in the middle of the night and sat up in bed because I thought I heard her call my name. Was she in trouble right then, and I'd sensed it? I don't know. It wasn't impossible, I believed, because I had the growing feeling that in some mysterious way I was linked to her.

Sometimes, just walking along the street by myself, I'd say: *If you need me, Catherine, send out some strong vibes.*

As much as possible, I completely separated her in my mind from Doomed. I didn't even think of her as *Mrs.* Stein.

On Thursday there was a notice outside the cafeteria ordering the football team to report for practice. Dr. Stein had arranged for us to have a substitute. He was a former professional named Bo Chayka, who was drying out at Lushing Brook. He had gone to college with Dr. Stein, but he looked much older because of his boozing. He gave us a lot of good ideas and he was full of slogans like "A winner never quits and a quitter never wins," and "If you play at a game, you won't win in a game."

That Saturday we beat Nottingham High. I don't know how we did it, because half the school didn't even show up.

That same afternoon Norman Putnam's father was buried, and a lot of the kids went to the funeral. I heard that Leah attended with Sophie and Doomed.

That didn't stop Doomed from sending his salesmen out to the stadium to hawk the new edition of REMOTE. It was the one saluting Charlotte Buff, who broke the heart of the German poet Goethe. Dave McGee was glancing through a copy of REMOTE in the locker room, after the game. Everyone else was dancing around pouring

Coke over each other's heads and celebrating the victory, but Dave looked miserable.

"This little newspaper has ruined my love life," he told me. "My girl doesn't want to go steady anymore. She says it's too straight for her. She says it is an-ac, anac, anac—"

"Anachronistic?" I said.

"Yes," he said. "What does that mean?"

"Out of date," I told him. "Belonging to another time."

"Do you realize what Doomed is doing to all of us, Alan?"

"I realize it," I said.

"Nobody's going steady anymore but you and Leah."

"Maybe that's anachronistic, too."

"I heard that Leah and Doomed are very palsy-walsy."

"They've become friends," I said.

"Yeah."

"Well, that's all they are. Leah's just going through a stage."

"Everyone's going through a stage," Dave said. "I never thought senior year would be like this."

It was then that I noticed a small box at the bottom of the front page of REMOTE. Above the box was the word *FLASH!* Inside the box it said:

We are proud to announce that Norman Putnam has just been appointed to our staff.

171

"Norman Putnam," I said. I'd been about to make some crack about there not being enough space in any newspaper for anything Norman Putnam would write, but I couldn't do it, because of what'd happened to his father.

"I noticed that," Dave said. "It's kind of freaky, isn't it? Since when are Norman Putnam and Doomed friends?"

"I don't have any answers anymore," I admitted.

We didn't even have a victory celebration that night. It wasn't just because of the funeral, and the fact a lot of kids felt down about Norman's father. It was more because there were a lot of secret rendezvous taking place: this one meeting that one to discuss love poetry for an evening (never to meet again); that one meeting this one to take a long walk around the lake (never to meet again). Some kids were just staying home to write letters to Box B or C, and some were waiting for telephone calls from Box Q or R.

The florists in town were even advertising in their windows:

WE HAVE ANEMONES!

I stayed in that night; it was the first Saturday night I could remember staying home. I worked on my composition "A Father I Know." I drew an old man with a scythe at the top of the paper. Then I began:

> *Of all the fathers I know, this one is the worst. When he's through with you, you're nothing, and everything that ever meant anything to you is meaningless. Even love will prove to be just a trap, after Father Time has his way....*

In the midst of writing this, I got up and went directly to the telephone. I dialed Leah's number and got Mr. Pennington.

"Is Leah in?" I said. I planned to simply say: *Okay, let's cut it out and be ourselves. I'm tired of acting, Leah.... I love you, Leah.*

"Why aren't you at Rushing Brook?" Mr. Pennington said.

"I don't have a drinking problem," I told him.

"Ha-ha-ha," he responded appreciatively. "But that's where Leah and Sophie are. There was a little dinner party there for Norman tonight. I thought you'd be there too, Alan."

"Well I'm not," I said. "Thank you, anyway."

Later my mother and grandfather came home from the movies, and we sat around for a while watching a rerun of a talk show on television.

At one point my mother said, "The Steins are truly lovely people. I heard that Catherine Stein has been just wonderful to poor Mrs. Putnam, taking her casseroles and having Norman out to dinner."

"Misery enjoys company," I said.

"What does that mean, Alan?" my mother said.

"I don't even know," I said.

"It's a strange thing to say. I can think of a lot of adjectives for Catherine Stein, but 'miserable' isn't one of them."

"You have to hand it to people of the Jewish persuasion," my grandfather said. "They have heart. Of all the people in this town who know the Putnams, the Steins know them least well, but Dr. Stein put the Rushing Brook limousine at their disposal. Complete with chauffeur."

"What's a limousine without a chauffeur?" I said snidely.

"What's your nose out of joint for?" my grandfather said.

My mother said, "You know, Dad, I don't think 'heart' has anything to do with religious persuasion."

"Besides," I said, "that term is laughable. Mrs. Stein thought it was funny the day I said 'someone of the Jewish persuasion.'"

"That's true," my mother agreed. "She called it 'cute.'"

"I'm in business in this town, in case you don't know it," my grandfather said, "and I'm not going to go around calling people Jews!"

"But they *are* Jews," my mother said.

"Except for her," I said.

My grandfather said, "I don't name-call."

I groaned and my grandfather shot me a dirty look. "Don't you name-call either, Alan."

"People call us Protestants," I said. "Is that name-calling?"

"I'm going to bed," my grandfather muttered. "I'm not looking for a fight, like some people."

When my mother and I were alone, she said, "Tell me something, Alan?"

I thought she was finally going to question me about the weekend with my father. In a way, I wanted her to. I guess I wanted her to behave like Leah, who knew me well enough to know you had to coax things out of me. But my mother was bent on honoring my privacy, because when I said "What do you want me to tell you?" she said "Don't you like the Steins? I know you don't take to the boy, but you like Dr. and Mrs. Stein, don't you?"

I shrugged. "I guess so."

"Then why all the sarcasm about the chauffeur and why call Mrs. Stein 'miserable'?"

"I heard Leah was out there for dinner tonight," I said. "I guess it just burns me up. How long can Leah keep this up?"

"If you love someone," my mother said, "you have to let them know it. Don't play hard to get. Love is a verb."

While I was trying to fall asleep that night, I tortured myself with all sorts of mean fantasies: Leah becoming bosom pals with Catherine Stein; Catherine Stein telling her she met me on the bus and I behaved like a twerp; Leah getting the whole story about the coach and Catherine Stein from Catherine Stein herself . . . and even Leah becoming strangely linked to El Unbelievable, as I felt myself linked to Catherine Stein.

Nowhere in my fantasy life did Doomed take part.

I thought over what my mother said about love being a verb. I decided I'd take the bull by the horns and corner Leah Sunday morning when she came to church. I got there early, because the Penningtons always arrived ahead of time.

After I'd been standing there about twenty minutes, I saw Mr. and Mrs. Pennington and Sophie coming up the walk. No sign of Leah.

I pulled Sophie aside and said, "Where's Leah?"

"Back in your old rut, hmm?" she sneered.

"Listen, Sophie," I said. "Just give me a straight answer this time, okay?"

Sophie pushed her glasses back on her nose and her lips tipped in a crooked grin. "Motivate me," she said. "I have no motivation for answering you. I haven't forgotten what you said about it not making any difference in El Unbelievable's life, whether he received a greeting card from me or the receptionist in Dr. Brewster's office."

"I was only joking," I said.

"Nobody ever jokes. There's always a seed of truth in every joke."

"I'm sorry about that remark," I said, choking back rage. "Where's Leah?"

"She won't be coming to church this morning," she said. "We had a gala evening last night, the most gala evening I can remember having ever. Leah never looked so radiant in her entire life."

"Where is she?" I said. "At the synagogue?"

I couldn't believe what had come out of my own mouth.

"The synagogue!" Sophie jeered. "You are so ignorant you should not be let out. The Jewish Sabbath happens to be on Saturday! *You* are why we are called WASPS!"

On that note, Sophie stormed away.

I realized, suddenly, why I'd made that remark. It brought me face to face with something I had refused all along to admit to myself. I was jealous of Doomed.

Seventeen

A few days before Thanksgiving, a package arrived for me from New York City. It contained the sports coat my father had bought me at Brooks Brothers, and this note:

> *Dear Alan,*
> *Your mother and I used to like the plays of Tennessee Williams. I don't know whether kids today are much interested in his work. But this is something I like from one of his works,* Sweet Bird of Youth:
> *'I don't ask for your pity, but just your understanding—not even that—no. Just for—your recognition of me in you, and the enemy, time, in all of us.'*
>
> > *Sincerely,*
> > *Ken Kinney*

I showed my mother the letter, after I told her the whole story of the weekend.

After reading the letter, she handed it back to me and asked, "How do you feel about it?"

"I don't recognize him in me at all," I said. (But it was a little eerie that he'd chosen something that had to do with the enemy, Time, just when I'd finished a composition about Father Time's destruction.)

"I don't think he means it that literally," she said. "I think he just means that we ought to all be able to see other people's sadnesses in our own experiences."

"I think it's just a big copout," I said. "He thinks a philosophical quotation is going to let him off the hook for being a louse. He gets away with it, too. Everyone seems to forgive him."

"You don't," my mother said.

"You bet I don't. I never will—not because of what went on in New York, but for walking out on you. I don't care how much passion he was suffering—it was his responsibility to stick by his vows. He's always been a copout."

My mother didn't pursue the subject. She said, "I have a call to make this afternoon for FLF. How about helping me out? Can you skip football practice?"

"There isn't any practice. Bo Chayka's gone home for the holidays."

Some newcomers had moved into an apartment

out on Palmer Avenue. My mother didn't know much about them, but she went ahead with the call anyway, so she could fill her monthly quota.

On the way there, in the car, I said, "How do people who love each other get to be so understanding? You seem to understand my father, and Pam seems to, and there doesn't seem to be any right or wrong—you just understand all the time."

"I wasn't that understanding of your father at the time, Alan. That came later."

"I guess the one thing you can't forgive in a marriage is if one partner is playing around," I said.

"It's pretty hard to forgive, yes."

"Particularly if it's the female partner, wouldn't you say?"

"Yes. Men find it harder to take."

"But some men, I suppose, manage to forgive it."

I was thinking of Catherine Stein and El Unbelievable.

My mother said, "Do you think Leah's involved with someone else, is that it?"

"Well, she's not having an affair."

"I didn't mean that. I meant, do you think she's attached to someone else?"

"A lot of the girls are freaky lately," I said. "A lot of the guys are too. Being attached to someone is going out of style."

"I doubt that," my mother said.

"You don't know what's been going on at school."

"It's just a fad, Alan."

"Some fad."

"Is the boy Duncan Stein?"

"Leah's friends with him, that's all."

"Do they date?"

"He's been helping Norman Putnam get over his father's death, and Leah and Norman and Sophie and him have been hanging around together."

"How do you feel about Leah?"

"She doesn't seem like someone I can count on anymore. She feels trapped, or something."

"I see."

"I don't care," I said. I didn't want my mother feeling sorry for me. "Leah's really just a kid. I'd prefer a woman. You know, someone you can protect."

"Protect?"

"Well. Women need protection, don't they?"

"Among other things," my mother said.

"Well, they do, don't they?"

"Yes . . . but that's not all."

We arrived on Palmer Avenue then, so we didn't pursue the conversation.

There isn't much to tell you about the people we called on, except that the man's name was Ralph Otis, and when my mother asked him his occupation, he said, "I'm the new coach at

Cayuta High. I thought you knew that."

"I didn't," my mother said. "What happened to Coach Luther?"

"I heard he resigned," said Mr. Otis. "That's all I know."

Then we went through the whole this-is-my-son-he's-on-the-team bit, and my mother went into her act, and we had Cokes and sat around making polite conversation for a while.

I couldn't concentrate on any of it. It really hit me then that the coach wasn't coming back. I'd thought he might apply for another job; I thought he might eventually leave Cayuta—but I never thought it'd happen *bang,* like that.

In my mind's eye I kept seeing his little Triumph in the parking lot at the airport. I wondered if it was still there. He had to come back, didn't he, at least to get his car, pack, do all of that? That Sunday afternoon at the Syracuse airport couldn't have been the last meeting ever between the coach and Catherine Stein ... could it?

Instead of riding back home with my mother, I got off in town and went to Murray's. There were a few kids hanging around there, and I told them about this Ralph Otis. It was a surprise to everyone. One of the guys had a car, and we piled in and drove by Coach Luther's house. I don't know what we expected to see, but we didn't see anything. His car wasn't in the driveway, of course; there was no sign of life.

"He'll be back," I said. "He's got to pack up."

"I wonder why he split so suddenly?" one of the guys said. "I know he hated our guts, but he couldn't have hated our guts to that extent!"

Someone else said, "That's why he was acting so nice those last weeks. He knew he was splitting."

"I don't think so," I said. "I think at the end he was changed by something."

The day before Thanksgiving, we learned that the coach's sister showed up in Cayuta with some professional movers, and loaded all his belongings on a van. His house was put up for sale.

That afternoon, ahead of schedule, Doomed turned in his composition, "A Father I Know," and Mrs. Tompkins read it to our English class. She thought so highly of it that she had copies mimeographed so everyone could have one.

A FATHER I KNOW

My father was a drunk when he met my mother. I was six years old. I don't remember my real mother at all. She died in childbirth. Now, I hardly remember my father when he was doing his heavy drinking, but I can recall him coming into my room very late at night, bumping into furniture and cursing. He would bear-hug me, still in his overcoat, with his breath reeking of whiskey. He would hold me so tightly that I hurt, and I tried to struggle loose. He would say, "Come on, now.

Come on, now. I'm not going to hurt you!"
and it would make him angry that I tried to
get away.

There is an old Beatle song that never became famous, written by Paul McCartney,
called "Maybe I'm Amazed." A line goes
". . . you pulled me out in time, hung me on
the line . . ." This is what my mother did for
my father.

My father was amazed, but even more
amazed was my grandmother.

My grandmother was amazed because my
mother was a shiksa, which is a word you
don't hear much in this neck of the woods. It
is a word describing a non-Jewish woman. It
is from the Hebrew, sheques, meaning "blem-
ish."

My grandmother considered my father
dead when he married my mother. So did all
of my relatives and many of my father's close
friends, all Orthodox Jews.

But that was when he became alive for me,
and my true memory of him was born then.

In Barbary Shore Norman Mailer wrote
"Love is simple to understand if you haven't
got a mind soft and full of holes. It's a crutch,
that's all, and there isn't a one of us doesn't
need a crutch."

The story of my father is truly the story of

my mother, who pulled him out in time.

There was only one thing I liked about Doomed's composition, and that was the revelation that he was not Catherine Stein's flesh and blood.

Everyone else (particularly the girls with the weeds pinned to their sweaters) thought Doomed was really heroic to write such a personal thing about his family.

To me, Doomed came off like a hypocrite. If love was a crutch that everyone needed, how did his REMOTE philosophy figure into the scheme of things? It seemed to me he was suddenly talking out of both sides of his mouth. On the one hand, love was something you needed in order to survive; on the other, true love didn't last.

Another thing that bothered me was the idea of Catherine Stein as a crutch. It sounded as though she just existed to complement El Unbelievable.

It all left a bad taste in my mouth, and I sat through my classes that afternoon remembering Catherine Stein crying beside me on the bus, and lighting one cigarette after the other, and trying to get her head together.

I was still thinking about her when I bumped smack into Leah, on my way to football practice after last bell.

"Well! Hel-*lo!*" she said.

"*You* look happy," I said.

"I guess I am, Alan."

"Good. Great!"

"*You* don't."

"I have a few minutes before I have to report to the gym," I said. "Do you want to talk?" I didn't even know what I wanted to say to her, anymore. My feelings about her jumped around like a stunt pilot's barometer—way up one minute, way down the next. The trouble was, when they were way up, I never seemed to be able to find her, and when they were way down, I'd see her . . . and make no effort to talk with her.

She moved over against the wall, hugging books to her bosom, and waiting for me to kick it off. On Thanksgiving day the team played its last game of the season, and Thanksgiving night there was always a dance in the gym. Parents often came, and other townspeople who'd supported the team; it was like a community dance.

I said, "I suppose you have a date for tomorrow night?"

"Yes. I do."

"Who with?"

"Dunc . . . Sophie's going with Norm. We're double-dating."

"What about us?"

"What *about* us?" she threw it back at me.

"How can you show up at the dance with

Doomed?" I said angrily. "You'll be in a class with Gwendolyn Graney, and Kim Lingerman, and every other little nobody he's taken out!"

"*I'm* not worried about my image," she said.

"I suppose you think I'm worried about mine?"

"You should be if you're not."

"What does that mean?"

"It means, how long are you going to coast along on your good looks, Alan Bennett? What have you ever *done?* Did you ever publish your own newspaper? Did you ever do anything for anyone but yourself?"

"He sells that newspaper," I said. "He's doing that for himself."

"You couldn't sell anything, much less dream up an idea like REMOTE," she said, "and you couldn't care less about other people! Where were you when Norman Putnam's father died?"

She had me there. I couldn't come up with an answer.

"You're the one who's Doomed," Leah said. "Not Dunc."

We won the game the next day.

I looked around the locker room for Dave McGee, hoping we could commiserate together for a while, since he was the only member of the team who seemed to care as much about his love life as football.

I found him under the shower, soaping his hair

and singing at the top of his lungs.

"Want to walk home together?" I called in to him.

"I can't, Alan. I'm going to my girl's for Thanksgiving dinner."

I started to leave and he called after me, "We'll see you at the dance tonight. Okay?"

"Are you going with her?" I shouted.

"Sure! We've patched things up!"

"Neat!" I said, with a sinking heart. "Neat."

After Thanksgiving dinner, I went up to take a nap, and to try and decide what I was going to do about the dance that night.

I couldn't just stay home. The team always went, every member. At a certain point in the evening, they asked the team to come out on the floor en masse, and receive a round of applause.

I didn't want to be the only one absent—everyone would know I wasn't there because Leah was there with Doomed.

I don't know what kind of a daydream I'd been walking around in, but right up until that confrontation with Leah in the hall, I'd thought something would happen at the last minute, and we'd go to the dance.

Maybe Leah had been right; maybe I was really all wrapped up in myself. But for someone who believed in ephemerality, Doomed seemed to be sticking like flypaper.

I went to the dance by myself. A few guys always went stag, but I never had. I tried to pretend I was having a great time, eyeing all the girls, cutting in on a dozen, smiling so much my mouth actually hurt.

But after Leah made her late, great entrance with Doomed, I couldn't keep up the act. I didn't feel like dancing or smiling or doing anything but rolling myself up into a ball to be buried in some hole in the ground.

I was hanging around the punch bowl making small talk with some of my grandfather's colleagues from Rotary, when I saw Catherine Stein heading in my direction. She was all in white, with her black hair piled on top of her head, smiling that smile of hers at me.

"Is this my dance, Alan?"

"Do you want to dance?"

"That's why I'm asking."

We danced to one of the few slow numbers the Grand Awfuls knew. At first I couldn't think of anything to talk about, and I couldn't seem to get her in step with me. I was hesitant about really holding her around the waist, and I was embarrassed because my palms were suddenly wet. All those self-conscious little things. And then we seemed to be gliding along just fine, and I became aware that we were making conversation quite easily, because she wasn't fooling around with small talk, which is hardest of all for me to manage.

". . . may think now that you'll never get over it," she was saying, "but I promise you, you will."

"I don't blame her for coming with Duncan," I said. "He's a very original guy, I guess. I guess I thought I could just coast along on my good looks . . . not that I'm so good-looking."

"Oh, you *are.*"

"We were just about at the end of things, anyway," I lied.

"Duncan wouldn't have butted in if there'd been any way he could have kept himself from it," she said. "I think it's been a shock to him, too."

"What has?"

"Falling in love," she said.

"*What* has?"

"Falling in love. I don't think anyone sets out to fall in love."

"Well, a little ephemeral love can't do much damage," I said.

"Dunc never really knew what he was talking about when he was advocating all that. He'd never been in love. He'd intellectualized it. Now he's experiencing it."

"Leah and I were just about at the end of things, anyway," I repeated, like some kind of windup doll.

Catherine Stein said, "You were so kind to me during our secret bus ride. You must have thought me very callous. I was so distracted."

"I didn't give it a second thought," I said. I was still digesting the idea of Doomed in love with Leah.

"When I saw you, as I came in the door tonight, I knew I couldn't pretend to you that I wasn't aware of what Duncan's doing."

"I'm glad you didn't," I said.

"Alan?"

"What?"

"If you ever feel like it, come out to Rushing Brook and we'll talk about writing. I'll introduce you to O. Henry, since you've never heard of him. He's not deep, but he's fun, and very big on trick endings."

"Of course there's no guarantee how Leah feels," I mumbled.

"Now *you're* not listening to *me*," she said. "And I understand."

For a few seconds, I turned and watched Leah and Doomed dancing together. Leah's eyes were closed and Doomed was pressed against her; they were hardly moving.

The rest of the evening was a blur. Out of the corner of my eye, at one point, I saw Sophie dancing with El Unbelievable, whose nose was still bandaged. I vaguely remember talking with Dave McGee and his girl. I vaguely remember some sort of scene created by Gwendolyn Graney, who left the gym sobbing "Duncan! Come back!"

I left before the last dance, and walked home by myself in the snow.

Something else happened that night, too.

When I finally did get home, Bo Chayka was sitting in our kitchen with my mother and grandfather, having a cup of coffee. On his way back from the holidays, his car had broken down in front of our house.

My grandfather was yawning and rubbing his eyes, and trying to keep up his end of the conversation while they waited for the tow truck.

My mother and Bo Chayka were very much awake and watching each other across the kitchen table.

Things end, and things begin, at different times for all of us.

Eighteen

That winter at C.H.S., everything went back to normal.

Under Norman Putnam's management, RE-MOTE failed. I doubt that anyone could have kept it alive, anyway. The idea of ephemeral love and unrequited passion had been crossed off as just another fad.

Practically everyone in the senior class was going steady but me, including Leah and Doomed.

Love had changed Doomed. He became Cayuta's star basketball player, and the editor of our yearbook. He seemed to change in another, more subtle way. It wasn't that he had become handsome—he hadn't magically grown hair, or even bought new eyeglasses. But there was a certain glow about him. He stood tall and walked in a new, sure way, and he was nearly always smiling. He was very popular by then, too.

Even though I had never shown any interest in the high-school drama club, I should have received the award that year for best actor. I had a full-time acting job that winter. I was playing myself. I hadn't been myself since the day I heard Leah and Doomed were a couple.

I went through the motions of living like an automaton—laughing (without hearing the joke) when everyone else laughed, down at Murray's; dating several girls for the basketball games on Saturday nights—continuing my old routine. But my daydreams were all of the past, when Leah was my girl; my head was stuck in Memory Lane, and I was beginning to think I was psyching out altogether.

One afternoon at the beginning of spring, I met Catherine Stein in the library.

"Is everything all right, Alan?" She knew it wasn't. I could tell by the way she looked at me.

"How are you?" I said, without answering her question.

"Oh, I'm fine," she said with a sigh. I knew everything wasn't all right with her, either.

She invited me to visit her some afternoon at Rushing Brook. I chose the following Thursday, because that afternoon the yearbook staff always worked after school. I didn't want Doomed around.

That Thursday visit was the first of many.

I never mentioned the coach's name, and neither did she. But I could tell from our conversations that she was filled with great sadness. If she'd ever guessed that I'd seen her with the coach that day at the Syracuse airport, she never indicated it.

We discussed books and took long walks together by the lake. I marked passages in books which I read to her during these meetings, and I stored up little sad occurrences I saw or heard about, to share with her. I had tuned in to the bittersweet tragedies of life: The sampler in the antique store window which said: *Those whose ships have n'er come in, will find a welcome here within*. . . . A painting I saw in an art book of a man weeping in a graveyard by a tombstone, while behind him a funeral was taking place, a lone woman standing in black before another grave. . . . A coffee mug I saw advertised in the back of a magazine, and on it the inscription: *Enjoy me before I grow cold.*

"You have such a melancholy side, Alan," she said to me once.

"I didn't use to."

"You have a Russian soul . . . have you read Dostoevski?"

I never had, but I began reading his novels, and getting very deep into my soul. I would memorize lines to recite to her, like these:

I saw that a tender feeling was blossoming in her heart, like a rose in spring and I could not help recalling Petrarch's saying, "Innocence is often but a hair's breadth from ruin."

I lived for those Thursday afternoons with Catherine Stein.

Gradually I began to drop out of the extracurricular activities at school. I didn't go out for baseball, or attend the tennis matches, or show up at Murray's after school.

When I saw Leah with Doomed, it didn't hurt anymore. I thought of Leah as this great girl I'd once gone steady with, but I was different since knowing Catherine Stein. I wanted a *woman;* I wanted a woman who had been through something, suffered, had a taste of life's pains.

One afternoon I said to Catherine Stein, "I've become an introvert. I could never go back to being the old rah-rah Alan Bennett. I guess I've matured. I don't even remember the past anymore."

"It's not wise to forget the past, though." She smiled at me in her wistful way. "They say that those who don't remember the past well are condemned to relive it."

I got the feeling she was thinking about her own past, when she'd pulled El Unbelievable out in time . . . and about what might have happened to her, if the coach hadn't left town. She might have gotten in too deep, trying to rescue another man from his misery. Obviously, she had let go before that happened, had forced herself to give him up. I think that's what I most admired about her. She'd had the strength to turn away—unlike my old man.

Yet I felt she was soft and vulnerable, and the time we spent together helped her through it all. I felt she needed me. The protective feeling I had toward her grew and grew. I thought of us as a kind of island, separated from the mainland by a deep, unspoken realization of what life and love were really all about.

I was determined to become a great writer because of her, and I was going to dedicate my first book to her.

A few times I admitted to myself that my feelings toward Catherine Stein weren't all that spiritual. I was very aware of her physical presence. I even had fantasies of making love to her. But on the rare occasions when I did admit that to myself, I told myself that wasn't what mattered. I couldn't help it if I was a normal male with normal male responses, but she meant something else to me, something more. She was not my idol, exactly, but my ideal.

For once in my life, my mother wasn't tuned into what was going on in my life. She was busy dating Bo Chayka. I was glad for her, although Bo Chayka was one of those hair-mussers too, who reached out for the top of my head everytime I went near him.

The only time I ever thought of my father was when I contrasted his running off with Catherine Stein's staying. His weakness; her strength.

As graduation came near, I was eager for my school days to be over. I wasn't comfortable with my classmates anymore. They seemed young and immature. I was also considering skipping college. There were many writers who'd never gone to college. Why should I waste four years when I could be living at home, writing a book? Sometimes I envisioned myself taking chapters of my book to Catherine Stein, discussing it with her step by step. In the fall, Doomed would be away. He was going to Yale.

Predictably, Doomed was our class valedictorian. It was announced a few days before the actual graduation ceremony, and I remember Catherine Stein referring to it during one of our walks.

"Yes, Dunc's going to be all right from now on," she said.

"Did you ever doubt it?"

"I wanted to be very sure."

"I wouldn't worry about him," I said.

"Who are you taking to the prom?" she asked.

I hated it when she said anything that had to do with school, or my mother, or any other subject which pointed up the fact we weren't contemporaries. I liked sticking to discussions of books and philosophy, or just silently walking along together.

I passed by the question with a shrug, and changed the subject to poetry.

But before she went along with the change, she managed to say, "I hope you're going, Alan. I'm going to be a chaperon."

I'd already suffered through a huge hassle with my mother over the fact I didn't want to attend the prom. After I heard Catherine Stein would be there as a chaperon, I *knew* I wouldn't go.

It got back to the matter of pointing up the fact of our age difference, and the fact I was this high school kid I never felt I was when we were alone together.

I didn't go. My mother said I'd regret it all my life—I don't know about that. But what I did, instead, went along with this new me I felt myself becoming. I took a flashlight, a copy of Dostoevski's *Notes from the Underground,* a blanket, and a bottle of wine, and I went up to the lake. I chose a spot where Catherine Stein and I had often sat watching the water. I read, sipped wine, and felt my Russian soul approve. I guess I thought a lot about her, too.

I still didn't call her Catherine to her face. I couldn't bear to call her Mrs. Stein, so I simply didn't call her anything, though she said my name often. I planned to start calling her Catherine at our next meeting.

My thoughts were seldom involved with my old friends. Things happened around me; they registered, but it was like hearing news about a small town you'd moved away from . . . El Unbelievable had a plastic surgeon carve out a new nose for him, and became as beautiful as ever, running here and there on his lecture dates, out of town more than he was in town . . . Norman Putnam won and accepted a scholarship to a private school, after his mother made plans to move to Wisconsin . . . Carleton Penner threw up on stage playing Dr. Throstle in the senior class production of *Berkeley Square* . . . Sophie got all A's and made an appointment with Dr. Brewster to be fitted for the new soft contact lenses.

As I drank wine by the lake, late that night of the prom, I drank a little good-bye-to-all-that toast. All that was fine, I muttered to myself, but none of them, including Leah, ever needed me.

Then I practiced the way I'd say it: "I think I'd better start calling you Catherine." . . . Or just "Hello, Catherine."

I was a little drunk when it dawned on me that, in a way, I'd traded places with Doomed. Here he was, going steady; here I was, into something not entirely unlike the philosophy preached in RE-MOTE.

The day after graduation, I went to the library to look up information on college correspondence courses. Before I announced to my mother that I didn't want to go away to college, I wanted to have some ammunition for my argument. I could work on a correspondence degree while I was working on my novel. I left the library all smiles, anticipating how surprised Catherine Stein would be when I told her I'd be around for a long, long time—she could count on it.

As I went down the library steps, I ran into Sophie. There were tears in her eyes.

I said, "I thought the new lenses didn't cause tearing?"

"My eyes aren't wearing the new lenses," she said, "or I wouldn't have stopped to talk to you. I didn't know it was you. I can't see too well."

"Now that we are talking, though," I said, "what's new with all you kids? Has Leah been accepted by Smith?"

"Don't play dumb!" she said. "You were her friend."

"I'm still Leah's friend, and I hope you'll tell her—"

Sophie interrupted. "I'm not talking about Leah? I'm talking about *her!*"

"Who?"

"Mrs. Stein," Sophie said. "Mrs. Stein has left Cayuta forever. Bag and baggage! Duncan told Leah about it this morning. What is this going to do to El Unbelievable? Here's a case of—"

I walked away without waiting to hear what it was a case of.

I walked the three miles from center-town to my house. I didn't want to get on a bus where I'd have to be with people.

I couldn't get Catherine Stein's voice out of my head.

Catherine Stein saying, "They say those who don't remember the past well are condemned to relive it."

Catherine Stein saying, "Yes. Dunc's going to be all right from now on. . . . I wanted to be very sure."

The more I remembered, the more it all fit together. I just hadn't been listening very well at the time.

I told myself it was probably a lucky thing. I wouldn't have to feel so responsible toward her, or sorry for her. I'd begun to lose my personality in hers.

So, Alan, that's the way the ball bounces, I told myself—it's just a good thing you weren't in love with her, or anything stupid like that.

I supposed I'd go to Syracuse, after all . . . and

meanwhile, find some kind of summer job.

I began to whistle as I walked down my street. It was one of those songs that always plays in elevators: "Que Será, Será"—whatever will be, will be.

When I got home, my mother was in the kitchen getting dinner.

"Is that you, Alan? We're just about to eat."

"Great!" I said. "I'm hungry."

"You seem to be in a good mood."

"I am," I said.

"Did you hear about Catherine Stein?"

"The whole thing," I said. "I don't want to hear it all again."

"But Bo told me the strangest part," she said. "He said there was never a fight between a patient and Dr. Stein. He said it was Coach Luther who broke Dr. Stein's nose. Bo said she's run off with—" Her voice trailed off at the sight of my face.

"I don't want to hear about it," I said. "It hasn't got anything to do with my life."

But there was nothing I could do about the tears suddenly streaming down my cheeks, or the sobs beginning to punch their way out of my insides.

Outstanding Laurel-Leaf Fiction for Young Adult Readers

☐ **A LITTLE DEMONSTRATION OF AFFECTION**
Elizabeth Winthrop **$1.25**
A 15-year-old girl and her older brother find themselves turning to each other to share their deepest emotions.

☐ **M.C. HIGGINS THE GREAT**
Virginia Hamilton **$1.25**
Winner of the Newbery Medal, the National Book Award and the Boston Globe-Horn Book Award, this novel follows M.C. Higgins' growing awareness that both choice and action lie within his power.

☐ **PORTRAIT OF JENNY**
Robert Nathan **$1.25**
Robert Nathan interweaves touching and profound portraits of all his characters with one of the most beautiful love stories ever told.

☐ **THE MEAT IN THE SANDWICH**
Alice Bach **$1.25**
Mike Lefcourt dreams of being a star athlete, but when hockey season ends, Mike learns that victory and defeat become hopelessly mixed up.

☐ **Z FOR ZACHARIAH**
Robert C. O'Brien **$1.25**
This winner of an Edgar Award from the Mystery Writers of America portrays a young girl who was the only human being left alive after nuclear doomsday—or so she thought.

Complete foreign language dictionaries for travelers, students, and linguists: